LOW KEY FALLIN' FOR A SAVAGE

J. DOMINIQUE

Cole Hart
SIGNATURE NOVELS

Low Key Fallin' For A Savage

Copyright © 2020 by J. Dominique

All rights reserved.

Published in the United States of America.

Mailing List

To stay up to date on new releases, plus get information on contests, sneak peeks, and more,

Go To The Website Below...

www.colehartsignature.com

TEXT TO JOIN

To stay up to date on new releases, plus get exclusive information on contests, sneak peeks, and more...

Text ColeHartSig to (855)231-5230

DESTINY

ere we go with this shit again. This was the first thing that came to mind as I stepped foot into the small ass two-bedroom apartment that I shared with my boyfriend, Dre. After dealing with rude customers, instigating co-workers and a manager that talked way too much shit for the last eight hours; I wasn't at all happy to see his ass still sitting in the same spot I'd left him in. Judging from the mess that surrounded him on the couch as he sat yelling at the game, it was clear that he'd only gotten up to use the bathroom and get some snacks.

"What's up, bae!" He greeted me without turning away from the screen. I rolled my eyes but grumbled back a reply.

"Hey."

Without stopping to try and speak any further, I headed towards the kitchen to find an even bigger mess. It looked like Dre had eaten out of every plate and bowl we owned. There was spilled milk on the counters, some red sticky shit that I assumed was kool-aid on the table, and the garbage was overflowing. If I didn't know any better, I would have sworn that he had a gang of niggas in our shit while I was at work. Unable to hold my tongue, I slammed my purse into one of the chairs and stormed back to the living room. I didn't stop walking until I stood right in front of the tv instantly gaining his attention.

"Yo- what you doing Destiny!" His face twisted in anger, and he jerked forward like he was ready to hit me for the interruption.

"Why the fuck you leave the kitchen like that Dre! It was clean when I left, and now it looks like you had 20 muhfuckas eating in there!" I hadn't even got the chance to take off my crusty ass Burger King uniform and relax before having to clean up behind somebody else. Your house was supposed to be your sanctuary, and yet half the time I barely wanted to step foot in mine. I watched his eye twitch in irritation, but I didn't back down. Although I often tried to avoid letting our arguments get physical, I wasn't afraid to go toe to toe with his ass. Don't get me wrong I didn't consider Dre to be a woman beater, even though he couldn't beat my ass if he tried, but a few times he'd attempted to hem me up, and I automatically reverted back to the days I watched my mama get beat up by her ex. I didn't tolerate none of that shit! I'd die before I let a nigga hit on me. Some could say that Dre abused me in other ways, I know my family damn sure did. They constantly accused him of using me for a place to stay and money to spend. While I didn't think he was using me, I could admit that he was taking full advantage of the situation, but every time I tried to leave him alone, he'd act as if I were doing him wrong and turning my back on him like everyone else. And even though I knew that wasn't true guilt still plagued me to the point that I let him stay every time. I was stuck between a rock and a hard place too because while I was trying to make the best of our situation, I was still fed up with it.

"That's what the fuck this shit over?" He frowned tilting his head to the side. "You act like Yo'Sahn's bad ass don't live here too! I bet you ain't ask that lil muhfucka!"

I narrowed my eyes at him, ready to go off. This was another one of his tactics, placing the blame for his shit on my 12-year-old son. Every time I asked him about anything wrong at the house, he brought Yo'Sahn into it. I didn't know if it was because of testosterone or what but they both had a deep disdain for the other, and I always felt like I was in the middle. Sighing I pinched the bridge of my nose and tried to calm down. This was definitely not how I'd planned to spend my time once I'd gotten off. I didn't want to argue, and I honestly didn't want to clean up the mess that had been made either.

"Where is he?"

"His ass ain't here! He came in after school and left right back out to go run the streets as usual!" He scoffed making me roll my eyes. He hadn't even realized that he'd just proven that Yo'Sahn, in fact, couldn't have fucked up the kitchen because he wasn't there long enough to do the damage I saw.

"So, how he do all that if he only came in and left right back out?" I gave him a pointed look, and he just stared back at me blankly. He was only stuck for a second before he popped up off the couch in a huff.

"Yo, you always take his side bruh! He could've done that shit this morning, hell he could've done it before he just left! Man fuck this, I'm out!" Angrily he pushed past me and stormed off to our bedroom with me right on his heels.

"So you really bouta leave cause I asked you a question Dreon?" I asked calling him by his full name as I watched him search for clothes in disbelief. As irritated and tired as I was, I couldn't help but admire how fine he was. Dre was caramel-skinned and tall with a slim build, which is exactly how I like my men. He kept his hair tapered on the sides with a curly Afro on top and his goatee lined to perfection. His resemblance to the actor Trevor Jackson was so strong that I honestly thought that's who he was when he approached me five years ago. Of course, as handsome as he was he had to have some bad traits. I'd caught him cheating at least twice, and his ass couldn't keep a job to save his life! The last time he'd punched a clock was a few months before, and he'd quit because they had him doing too much heavy lifting. He always thought that he could make more money selling weed, so I'd put him on and he would do good for about two weeks before he'd completely fall off. I didn't know much about selling weed, but I did know that smoking your own shit didn't make you any money, and that's exactly what he would do while I was at work. A month ago he'd gotten some work from an unknown plug, but I honestly hadn't seen the fruits of it. He looked just as broke as he always did, but that wasn't my issue at the moment, so there was no point bringing it up.

By now he'd pulled on a pair of gray sweats over his basketball shorts and was in the process of putting on his hoodie. He still hadn't answered verbally yet, but the fact that he was still getting dressed; let me know that leaving was exactly what he planned to do.

"Really?" I stopped him from leaving the room with a hand on his chest.

"Yeah, really! I ain't got time for this shit!" He grabbed me up by my arms and roughly pushed me against the door and out of his way. "I'm going to my granny's." He tossed out over his shoulder as he disappeared down the hall. A few seconds later the door slammed letting me know he was gone. Annoyed with the whole situation, I pulled my phone from my back pocket so that I could call Yo'Sahn to try and see where his little ass was. I already knew that Dre was lying, so I wasn't even going to question him about it, but I did want to know where he went.

"Wassup ma?" He answered on the third ring, and I breathed a sigh of relief. Yo'Sahn was really a good boy, but lately, I'd been noticing a small change in him. It was like he was hardening before my eyes or maybe he was just growing up on me, and I wasn't ready.

"Where are you? You didn't ask me if you could go outside

today." My tone was light as I moved about the room getting prepared for my shower.

"Awwww ma come on why you tryna treat me like a baby?" I could hear the frown in his voice, and I had to hide my laughter. "I'm at Jayden's crib tho, he got the new 2k." He huffed and the faint sound of the games controller in the background confirmed that for me. I didn't mind him hanging out with Jayden. He was into all of the same things as Yo'Sahn, basketball, football, and video games. They both did pretty well in school, and I knew that his mama was doing her best to raise him right. In a city that damn near groomed little boys to be thugs from the moment they got their first chest hair I was extremely appreciative that my son was not falling into the same pattern as a bunch of these other little niggas. By now, I'd finished undressing and wrapped my short, terry cloth robe around my body. I made my way to the tiny bathroom that we all shared with the phone tucked between my ear and shoulder.

"Well, okay. Don't stay out too late Yoshi. You need to be your ass back in the house before it gets dark. You know how ignorant these niggas get when the sun goes down." I called him by the nickname I'd given him as a baby knowing that he hated it.

"I'm almost a man ma, you can't be calling me that baby stuff!" He whined making me giggle. My son was the most important person to me in the whole world. He was the reason I worked two jobs and strived as hard as I did.

"Well you gone always be my baby so I'll call you whatever I want."

The sound of the front door slamming shut had me rushing him off the phone with a quick goodbye because I didn't want him to hear Dre and me going at it again. For sure he would try and run his little ass home and jump in it, and I always tried to keep him away from shit like that, which was the reason I was no longer with his father Antonio. We had been high school sweethearts, and he had taken my virginity, which was how I'd gotten pregnant in the first place. As young as me and Antonio were we tried to make things work, but the stress of life and fatherhood came down hard on him. Not only was he out constantly falling in the next bitches pussy but he often took his failures out on me, and like I said before I wasn't with any of that abusive shit. After I left with my baby he tried for a while to force me back, but eventually, he left me alone, and unfortunately, he decided to leave Yo'Sahn alone too. As much as I wanted him to be a father to our son, that never stopped me from providing, and I'd been doing so for the last six years.

Rolling my eyes, I set my phone on the dresser and made my way to the front of the house ready for round two, but once I cleared the hallway, I instantly froze in place. Two men stood there holding guns pointed at Dre, who was cowered on the floor. They didn't notice me right away, so they were still talking to him as I frantically tried to think of a way out of this situation.

"So, let me get this straight. *You* came to *me* to eat, and instead of heeding the multiple warnings I gave you about playing with my money you thought that it'd be smart to run off with my shit?" The bigger of the two asked kneeling down in front of Dre with a nasty scowl.

"I swear I-I got the money! It's just not here!" Dre squawked fearfully. I'd never seen him so scared before. He usually had the persona of a man that would go toe to toe with the devil himself especially when me and Yo'Sahn were concerned, but seeing him now I realized he wasn't as tough as he tried to seem.

"Man Eazy, this nigga lying! Just let me do his ass!" The other guy grumbled obviously tired of the back and forth.

"I'm not lyin' man, I swear!"

I watched in horror as the one they referred to as Eazy cocked his pistol. Neither man had their faces covered, so I was sure that they didn't intend on leaving any witnesses. As quietly as I could, I attempted to exit the room with my eyes still trained on them. If I could just get to the small gun that I kept in my closet, maybe I could get us out of whatever mess Dre had brought to our home.

"Please Eazy m-my girl here don't do this shit! I can get you the money!" I stopped my backwards trek and looked at him in disbelief. He'd basically just sold me the fuck out, and both men turned in my direction instantly ending any chance I had of going to the back. The one that was ready to shoot Dre turned his gun on me taking me in from head to toe.

"Damn nigga this you?" He chuckled looking back at Dre, with the gun still pointed my way. "I find that hard to believe, but bring yo ass on in here next to yo man." His tone was mocking, and I didn't find shit funny.

"Ayite, but take that damn gun off me," I said and sucked my teeth as I inched into the room. We stared each other down with him never lowering his weapon and me moving slowly until Eazy finally stood and gave him a short nod, which made him grudgingly put the gun down to his side. With it no longer pointed at me, I felt comfortable enough to take my eyes off of him and focus my hatred towards Dre. It took everything in me not to kick him when I made it to his side and took a seat on the couch. I crossed my smooth brown legs to keep from hitting Dre as he continued to plead his case without turning my way. He knew better than to look at me! My damn son could have been here, and he obviously wasn't gonna try and defend us. I rolled my eyes as I listened to him lie through his teeth about having the money until he mentioned the small safe in our bedroom. All of the restraint I'd been holding on to left my body, and I jumped on top of him punching and slapping him anywhere I could, no longer fearing the two niggas before us with guns.

"You bitch ass nigga, that's my money!" I growled as he attempted to block my blows weakly. He knew that the money I had in that safe was important. I'd been saving for six months so that my sister and I could put a deposit down on a salon. That and my son were the only reason I was holding on to the two dead-end jobs I had. Dre knew this, and instead of taking responsibility for his fuck up, he volunteered my hard earned money. If I wasn't done with him before I was definitely done now.

"We ain't got time for this shit! Get her ass off him Juice!"

"Hell naw! She fuckin that nigga up! Damnnnn!" I didn't even have time to relish in the fact that I'd busted Dre's nose before I was pulled away still swinging wildly.

"Aye shorty, chill yo lil feisty ass out! I ain't that nigga I'll slap the shit out you real quick. I don't give a fuck how fine you is!" Something about his tone had me calming down enough for him to put me down onto my feet, but he didn't remove his arm from around my body. As I stood trying to catch my breath, Eazy eyed me curiously before turning his attention back on Dre who sat holding his nose. "Damn man! How yo bitch got more heart than you?" The one holding me questioned still not releasing me from his grip. I didn't appreciate him calling me a bitch, but despite the humor he'd found in this I knew he'd no doubt make good on his threat, so I remained quiet.

"I've wasted enough time in here, I'ma give yo ass a week to bring me my money or my work Dre. That's seven days nigga! If I don't have one or the other I'm comin' here and airing this bitch out, then I'ma go to Ms. Ethel's house and do the same. And I don't give a fuck who in there!" Eazy threatened tucking his gun back in his waist and giving a nod towards the door. "Come on Juice."

He strolled away without giving Juice a chance to object, even though he let out a groan, making it clear he didn't agree with the decision. Juice let his arm linger around me for a second longer, before finally letting me go and stepping away and just like that they were gone. I shook away the mild sadness

I felt from not feeling Juice's strong arms holding me and went to stand over Dre, who still hadn't moved.

"You can get yo shit and leave right behind them niggas!" I snarled meaning every word I said. Him trying to give away my hard earned money was the last straw for me! I was done riding for a nigga that wouldn't even walk for me! Ignoring the look of shock on his face, I left his ass there on the floor, looking stupid and went to finally start my long awaited bath. If he knew what was good for him he'd be gone before I was done or I was going to do us all a favor and shoot his ass myself.

DREAM

"*O*h hell naw! I know you fucked that nigga up!" I gasped trying hard to keep my voice down as my sister filled me in on what had just happened at her house. I'd never liked Dre. He was the type of nigga to lay up all day while his woman went to work and took care of the household, but still walk around with his chest puffed out like he was the man. I'd been telling her for years to leave his no good ass alone, but it was like she couldn't see what everyone else saw. Even my nephew knew that nigga wasn't shit and I couldn't say I blamed Yo'Sahn for the hell he gave him.

"I busted his nose, but one of them pulled me back before I could really get in his ass!" I could hear the frown in her voice, and although I was happy that she got a hit off on him I was still pissed that I wasn't there to get me in a lick or two.

"Damn I wish I would've been there!" I grumbled.

"Ahem!"

I looked up and my words got stuck in my throat as I stared into the sexiest pair of eyes I'd ever seen on a man. They were chocolate colored, with a thick set of lashes that I couldn't help but envy. Even as he squinted down at me in frustration, I couldn't stop myself from ogling him enough to get my mouth to work. He was tall, towering over my desk at at least 6'3, and the color of mahogany with a set of deep waves and a full shiny beard. He easily put me in the mind of Don from Black Ink Crew.

"You gone stop eye fuckin me and do yo job, or do I need to go find Sherice myself?" He finally spoke and brought me out of my nasty thoughts.

"Ima call you back bitch," I mumbled hanging up on her mid-sentence. Clearing my throat, I stood and smoothed out the black wraparound skirt I was wearing before extending my hand. "I'm so sorry Mr….?"

"King." He filled in the blank for me, and the name was definitely fitting. Almost as soon as he closed my hand up in his, I felt a jolt of electricity that had my eyes widening in shock.

"Elijah!"

My boss Sherice appeared out of nowhere, and despite the smile plastered on her face, I could tell that she wasn't happy. I snatched my hand out of his and backed up just in time to avoid being knocked out of the way by Sherice who jumped right in front of me and planted a deep kiss on Elijah's lips. I should have known that he was there for more than just business. He was just Sherice's type ……just like all the other ones that frequented the office for her. I rolled my eyes and made my way back around my desk suddenly pissed off.

If you can't tell I couldn't stand this bitch. In the three years that I'd been working for her, I might as well have been running her business myself. All Sherice really did was cut checks and put on for her rich ass daddy whenever he decided to slide through, while I was meeting with clients, showing homes, and making sells with no commission. She had a rotation of three other niggas who stopped by a few times a week, and now she had this fine ass man here too. I couldn't help being a little jealous about a lazy scandalous hoe like her constantly winning in life while I was stuck working under her and barely getting acknowledged for my hard work. Thankfully, I wouldn't have to be subject to her bull shit for too much longer. Destiny and I had been saving our money up to start a makeup and hair salon. I'd gotten all of the small items that we'd need, and I was already looking for furniture. All I had to do was continue to bite my tongue in this bitch's presence for just a little while longer, because despite everything that I hated about my job I couldn't deny that I was paid better than most.

"I missed you baby." She cooed tangling herself in his arms and putting on a big ass show for me and every other female present. Bile rose up in my throat as I tried unsuccessfully to tune them out.

"Oh yeah? I missed yo ass too." Even though I could hear the smile in his voice, I looked up anyway so that I could witness it with my own two eyes. Regardless of who he gave his affection to, there was nothing sweeter than a man in love. However, Mr. Elijah King had his eyes on me while Sherice hugged him tightly completely unaware. Instead of engaging with this fool I averted my eyes back to the files on my desk which garnered a chuckle from him. He obviously was a hoe himself, so maybe he deserved the treatment that he was getting. I found myself wishing that the smooth jazz station that they played throughout the office was just a little bit louder so that I could tune out their lovey dovey banter, but it seemed like it was on the lowest setting today.

"I got something for you, but it was too big to bring up so you gone have to come outside to get it."

"What! Another gift!" Sherice squealed in excitement and clapped her hands together like a child. "Dream.....Dream! Go and get my coat from my office!" She ordered once she had my attention. As bad as I wanted to tell her to kiss my entire black ass, I nodded with a tight-lipped smile and headed back to retrieve her coat. Behind me I could hear her talking shit about

12

me being a lousy employee when she knew damn well I did her job and my own.

The second I was behind closed doors, I took a few calming breaths and reminded myself of why I needed this job. That was all it took to get my head right, and by the time I returned to my desk with her gray, Luxury Sentaler fur-lined Alpaca coat, I was calm, cool, and collected. She quickly snatched it out of my hands and slipped it on. I couldn't even lie she looked damn good in it. Her shapely figure was accentuated even behind the thick fabric. She looked like she had just stepped off the cover of a magazine with her flawless honey-toned skin, and model-like features. If the realtor business didn't work out she could definitely walk some runways.

She flipped her long Brazilian weave out of her collar smiling wide like she'd just won the lottery. I guessed I would have been cheesing too if I had a fine ass man like that bringing me presents that were too big to come up in the elevator. I watched as they began to walk away with a neutral expression, unlike the other thirsty ass hoes in the office who were damn near drooling and green with envy. At the last minute, Sherice turned around with a sly smirk.

"Y'all might as well come on too! I know y'all are dying to know what I got, but hurry up cause I'm not trying to wait!" The way these heffas started throwing on their coats, you would have thought somebody was outside giving out free shit. I held in the need to call them out and elected to just sit my ass down so that I could call my sister back. The distraction known as Elijah had taken my mind off of our conversation, and I really wanted to hear the end of her story. "Don't you want to come too *Dream?*"

The way she emphasized my name and the narrowing of her eyes told me that wasn't really a question, so I gathered up my coat and followed them all down mumbling obscenities under my breath the whole time. I worked directly with Sherice, so I got it worse than anybody else having to listen to her constant bragging. The last thing I wanted to do with my time was watch her flaunt her and one of her sponsor's wealth in my face. While they all guessed what her surprise could be, I pulled out my phone and scrolled Instagram.

I was the last one out of the building intentionally, pissed as soon as the cold ass Chicago air disrespectfully slapped me in the face. We stood huddled up on the sidewalk as a car rolled up completely covered in wrapping paper. Sherice excitedly let out another high pitched squeal once it came to a stop right in front of her and a guy that strongly resembled Elijah stepped out. A flash of annoyance crossed her face, at the sight of him, but it disappeared just as quickly when she remembered that she had a surprise coming.

"Baaaaabyyyy! You got me a car!"

"Gone head check it out," Elijah told her with a slight nod. He grinned unmoving as his brother took Sherice's spot next to him, and she ran off to open her present. I returned to my scrolling hoping that this little display would end soon so that I could go back inside of the warm building, while everyone else oooh'd and ahhh'd. At the sound of the wrapping paper coming off and confused murmurs, I tore my eyes away from my phone's screen. Underneath all of that shiny red paper was Sherice's midnight blue Porsche, filled to the brim with Louis Vuitton luggage.

"Ummm, are we going away?" Sherice asked skeptically. By now my undivided attention was on the pair, and the look of love that was once on Elijah's face was long gone. In its place was unmistakable anger, which she didn't seem to notice because she was too busy eying the luggage hard.

"Naw y'all ain't going nowhere, but you is hoe!" The other guy shouted, and I noticed him holding his phone out obviously recording her.

"What the fuck is he talking about Eazy! Is that my damn

luggage!" She shrieked, and just that fast this whole thing became much more entertaining.

"Hell yeah it's yours! Bitch you been cheating on my brother with a nigga named Hubert! We ain't letting that shit slide hoe! Yo ass is done!" I tried unsuccessfully to hold in my laughter as he went in on her. The look of defeat on her face was priceless, and it had me pulling up my camera app so that I could keep this moment forever.

"What are you even talking about? I don't know anybody named Hubert! Eazy you've got to believe me! Why are you letting him talk to me like this?" Sherice grabbed ahold of his wool trench as fake ass tears poured from her eyes. I didn't know of her messing around with a Hubert, but I wouldn't put it past her to have one in her damn roster. By now the crowd had grown as strangers joined us and made the situation that much more embarrassing.

"I just told you bitch-!"

"Calm yo ass down Jeremiah." Elijah held up a hand cutting his brother off. "I got it from here. I know about the other men you've been fucking with Sherice, it ain't even a need to lie. Now, I did you the courtesy of having your clothes packed and brought to you as well as your car. Just so that you don't have a reason to ever come by my crib again, because if I see yo ass again I can assure you I won't be so nice and we both know what I'm capable of....right?" His voice changed to a dangerously low pitch and his eyes blackened as he leaned forward so that he was inches from her face.

"Y-yes." Sherice nodded frantically damn near shaking from his threat.

"Good, I'm glad we got that understood." A cocky smirk came over his face as he backed away from her. "Oh yeah, give my number to yo receptionist." He added before walking away. My eyes bucked as a mixture of glee and surprise came over me, but that shit disappeared once Sherice found my face through the mix of people standing around. They parted like the Red Sea for her as she walked through and straight into my face.

"I bet you think you're real cute, huh? Well now you're cute and fired bitch!"

Almost as if they knew what was coming, two of my co-workers held me back while she stormed off. I angrily shook them away from me after she'd disappeared into the building and tried to calm myself down so I wouldn't go up there and beat the brakes off her ass. That fine ass nigga had come and shook up my whole damn day, and then he got me fired! I couldn't even believe this shit, and there was really no point in fighting her because even if I did stay, she would no doubt make the working environment too uncomfortable to tolerate. I hadn't planned on having to move up the timeline on our business *Lashes & Lace,* but God must have had it in store for me. I just hoped that it all worked out in the end.

EAZY

A couple of weeks had passed since I'd aired out Sherice's hoe ass in front of her staff and even though I knew she wasn't going to give my number to old girl I was still disappointed that I hadn't heard from her. No doubt she was just the type of woman I needed after dealing with Sherice for so long. It was still hard to believe that she'd been able to get one over on a nigga like me. I'd met her about four years ago when I'd been looking to purchase my first home. Sherice had been the realtor and the façade that she'd put up made her seem smart, funny, and most importantly, trustworthy. She was a boss just like me, and she wasn't ratchet as hell like some of the bitches I was used to. I could've never known how scandalous she really was though, because she made sure to put her best foot forward. She cooked for me, cleaned, helped me with some investment properties, I mean she was everything.

Not to mention she looked good as fuck and the sex was amazing. At the age of 29, I could appreciate all of those qualities, but I wasn't ready to commit. I wasn't out here wild like my little brother or nothing, but I kept me a woman or two in rotation the few times she wasn't available to me. I never lied about the other females I kept around, and she seemed to understand which gave her another point in my book. So, fast forward a couple of years, and I was trying to make our shit more serious. I was getting older and making more money than I could ever spend alone. It only seemed right that the next step was marriage. Despite knowing that I didn't *love* Sherice, I still wanted the same thing that my parents had, the kind of love that lasted decades. The fact that Rachel King never liked her from the moment I brought her to Sunday dinner should have told me something. My mama was usually a good judge of character, but I'd chalked that shit up to her just being overly suspicious. In our line of work, everything and everybody was questionable. My parents may not have been in the streets, but they were raised there, and they knew the game. They'd tried their hardest to keep Juice and me away from those very same streets, but it was like the more they tried, the more determined we were to be what they didn't want us to be. Honestly though the shit just came so naturally, you would never think that our parents were middle class, working folks. Our pops had been working at the post office for as long as I could remember and our mama owned her own hair salon.They both made a decent enough living to provide us with everything we needed and then some, but it just wasn't enough to stop us from falling into the trap of fast money.

Anyway considering that they'd both grown up on the rough ass south side of Chicago, they knew that you couldn't trust just anybody and while I could peep out some snake shit when it involved my business or my money the shit hadn't worked with Sherice. Who would have thought this whole time that the nigga she was telling everyone was her father was really her damn husband! It was a marriage of convenience on both their parts from what my guy told me. She wanted wealth, and he wanted a trophy wife that was half his age and was cool with her doing her dirt on the side. I don't know where I fit into all of that, but I was happy as fuck that I'd dodged that bullet.

"Bro this the funniest part! Look at her face!" Juice cackled holding his phone up for our homie Trell and a few other niggas that we balled with every month. I walked up to the bleachers where they sat and tossed my gym bag down as they all fell out laughing to the sounds of Sherice going off.

"Nigga you ain't tired of watching that shit yet?"

"Hell nah! That was some of the funniest shit I ever seen man! Real shit I should've sent this to the shade room!" Juice barely looked at me, he was so engrossed in how my break up played out. I couldn't lie the shit had been kind of funny when he came to me with the idea and even the way it played out had been hilarious but it was getting old at this point.

"Who the fuck is Hubert nigga?" Trell asked holding his stomach while cracking up. The question sent the rest of them silly ass niggas into another fit of laughter, and I gritted my teeth annoyed.

"Shiiiit I don't even know! I saw that shit on Instagram but she fucking some old nigga his name bout is Hubert!"

"Man all y'all niggas immature as fuck, is we bouta play or y'all gone sit over here giggling like some bitches?" I threw the ball I'd brought at Trell, and he caught it before it could connect with his chest.

"Awww this nigga mad y'all." He grinned standing up and tucking the ball underneath his arm as he came down the bleachers to stand beside me. Trell was the closest thing me and Juice had to a brother. We'd grown up together, and he was the only person besides Juice that I trusted with my life. That and our history was the only reason that I didn't hit his ass in the mouth for talking shit. The other three niggas there had shut the fuck up seeing that I wasn't in the mood for the bullshit.

"I'd be mad too if my bitch was out here picking up niggas at the nursing home and shit!" Juice cracked coming down to join us with Chad, Don, and Ant right behind him. "And you let all yo hoes go just to end up with one! You better call they ass back and tell em you changed yo mind!"

"Haha! Keep talkin' shit I'ma call yo bitch nigga!"

"Shiiit which one you want? I don't love these hoes!" He shrugged, and I knew he was dead ass serious. I wouldn't want nothing to do with any of the females on Juice's roster though. I was pretty sure half of them worked at a strip club or was unemployed, and the other half had rocks for brains. Sherice may have been a sneaky ass hoe, but she had a good head on her shoulders, and she made her own money.

"I'm just talkin, you know damn well I wouldn't fuck none of yo bitches with his dick." I frowned jutting my thumb in Trell's direction. Juice was just as reckless with his dick as he was with his life and I wanted no parts of that shit. He shrugged again because he never cared about my opinion on females. When he said he don't love these hoes, he was for real. He intentionally messed around with bitches that he saw no future with outside of sex. It was like he sought them out to avoid any real connection, but he'd been like this since high school. I thought that maybe it was just that phase that teenage boys go through where all they care about is getting their dick wet, but now the nigga had me wondering if there was something else.

"More bitches for me!" He waved me off. "Let's get this game started though I got some shit to do." Glad that the conversation had been dropped I moved to the middle of the court stretching as I walked. Our teams were always the same, me, Juice, and Trell against Chad, Don, and Ant. We'd been coming to the Y to play for the longest and nobody ever played during the same time that we did, so we always had the court to ourselves.

We had already played a few rounds when the sound of the door slamming shut brought all of our attention to a couple of little niggas that had just entered. They were dressed in regular street clothes, so it was clear that they weren't there to ball.

Silence filled the gym as we all stood staring them down and trying to catch our breaths. I could tell they both were afraid, but the taller of the two was the one with the heart. As if he was the spokesperson his friend gave him a slight shove in our direction, and he looked back at that nigga with a mug before settling his gaze back on me.

"Man what the fuck y'all lil niggas want!" Juice barked wiping sweat from his forehead. His patience was thin, and although mine was too, I had a bit more tolerance when it came to children. I might not have liked them little muhfuckas like thats but I could handle a conversation with one.

"Juice man chill, let lil man get it out." At this point I was interested in what he may have had to say, while my brother was immediately on the defensive and with good reason. These days they even had elementary school kids out committing hits, so his worry was warranted, but that wasn't the vibe I was getting from the boy. He cleared his throat, and a hardened look covered his face.

"I wanna be put on." He asserted, holding his chin high and folding his hands in front of himself. I even noted the added bass to his voice as I took him in. This kid couldn't have been no more than 14, and he was coming to me to ask for some work. I was a little uncomfortable for more reasons than one, and that caused a slight chuckle to come out as I eyed him. The fact that he knew enough about the streets that he came to me was a little unsettling. Also, he was dressed in name brand from head to toe, with the latest Jordan 12s on his feet, that meant that he was either already into some shit or his family worked hard to provide for his little ass. Whether I wanted to or not, I couldn't disregard how much of myself I saw in him, and that alone had me wanting for him to go a different way.

"What's yo name shorty?" I asked stroking my beard.

"Yo'Sahn." Again he spoke firmly, but I could tell that he had relaxed a little.

21

"Yo'Sahn, that's a cool name. How old are you?"

That question had him looking nervously between me and the other men in attendance before he focused back fully on me.

"I'm ....twelve."

"Ahh hell naw! Get yo lil ass outta here man! I knew this was some bullshit when you said yo name is the same as Herbo's son!" Juice voiced. I hadn't realized that he'd come over to where we were and was standing beside me. I gave him a warning look, and he sucked his teeth irritably. "What? I know you ain't bouta entertain this lil nigga!" He huffed side eying me like I was crazy before walking off when he realized that I was about to do just that.

"Come holla at me man." I motioned for Yo'Sahn to follow me over to the bleachers, ignoring the protests of my guys in the process. I led the way and took a seat all the way at the top to try and give us some privacy. "You already been working?" I asked as soon as he sat down a few inches away.

For the first time since he'd stepped foot in the gym, his voice was unsure when he replied. "Nah, but I need the money so I know I'll be good at this shit. I'm just tryna help my mama out. She doing her best but we still struggling, all she do is spend her money on bills and me, and by the time she done it ain't nothin' left. Her bum ass nigga ain't doin' it, and neither is my father, so I'm gone step up and take care of her for once." He watched Juice and the other guys as they took turns shooting the ball and dunking it. I was honestly surprised at how mature he sounded for someone so young, but I was sure that his mama wasn't working as hard as she was to take care of him just for him to turn around and sell drugs.

I didn't say nothing right away because really I was at a loss for words. I could see that he was hungry and ready to put some work in, but I didn't want to set him on the same path as myself.

"Aye look, I understand you need money, but let me be the first to tell you that this ain't the life you want." He gave me a look like he didn't believe me, and snorted in response. "Nah man for real, this shit ain't as glamorous as it seems." His face fell at my words, but I just couldn't allow myself to lead him down such a destructive path. "How bout I hook you up with another lil gig? You can still make some ends, and it'll be legit."

"Real shit?" He instantly brightened up and smiled looking at me expectantly, and I chuckled at his enthusiasm.

"Real shit, but you gone have to watch all that cussing and shit, you still a shorty and if my mama hears that I got you out here talking foul she'd fuck us both up." He nodded his understanding with a wide grin before dapping my outstretched hand.

"You mind if I catch a ride home, it's already dark as fu- I mean dark as heck, and I know my OG gone be on one if I try and wait for the bus." The anxiety that flashed across his face was one I was all too familiar with because me and Juice used to have to bring our asses in by a certain time too or else it'd be a guaranteed ass whoopin'.

"I got you," I told him easily, already smiling in pride at how he had corrected himself. We walked back down the bleachers, and I snatched up my bag, immediately reaching inside for my ringing phone.

"Aye bossman you got a problem." Was the first thing I heard when I answered the call from Big Boy, one of the niggas I paid to keep security at my house. I felt my brows dip, displaying my confusion at what he was saying. This was another downside to my chosen career. I could never trust anybody, even with my home. Of course, I never brought shit there, but that didn't mean niggas wouldn't run up in it.

"Nigga *I* got a problem, or *you* got a problem? You the one supposed to be securing my shit!"

"I was- I mean I am, fuckin Sherice got past the gate and inside the house. By the time I realized it she'd already trashed yo shit-." He stammered only adding to my irritated mood.

23

"Where is she?"

"I put her in the truck, and I got Moony watching her."

"Keep her there! I'm on my way!" I ended the call before he could say anything else and released a deep sigh as Yo'Sahn eyed me. "I gotta go handle something real quick lil man, but I'm gone have my brother drive you ayite, you got a phone?"

"Yeah." He bobbed his head up and down and pulled out an iPhone 6 with a damn near shattered screen. I took it so I could add my number deciding not to say anything right then because I was in a rush, but I made a mental note to replace it for him.

"Yo Juice!" I called out grabbing my brother's attention. Him and them other niggas were still tossing around the ball and hadn't even realized that I was preparing to leave. At the sound of his name, he came running over followed by Trell.

"What's up?"

"I gotta go take care of something at the crib, I need you to take Yo'Sahn home for me-."

"The fuck! Why I gotta take his lil ass? Send Trell, and I can ride with you." Immediately the concern that had been on his face had turned into irritation. I handed Yo'Sahn back his phone unbothered by the outburst. Juice could bitch and moan if he wanted to, but after the way he acted at Sherice's office I wasn't taking his ass with me for anything concerning her.

"Nigga cause I told you too, Trell can roll with me. And try to hurry up cause it's getting late." I gave Yo'Sahn another pound and then tapped Trell so we could leave while Juice stood there silently fuming. Regardless of his feelings, he was going to do it, he'd just have an attitude while he did. Either way I ain't care. I needed to get home and handle Sherice, hopefully for the last time.

When I pulled through my wrought iron gate, I could see Moony struggling with a disheveled looking Sherice. I barely put my truck in park before hopping out with Trell by my side. She was so busy acting a fool that she didn't realize I'd pulled up until I was within arm's reach of the melee. As soon as Moony let her little ass go, she punched him dead in the mouth.

"Keep your hands off me nigga!" She howled ready to attack again, not even knowing that he was on the verge of fucking her up. I quickly snatched her up, pulling her out of harm's way. Sherice went to swing on me too, but once she realized who I was she calmed down slightly.

"Aye, thanks Moony man. I got it from here." I told him trying to diffuse the situation. The look in his eyes let me know he was five seconds from shooting her ass right there, and I couldn't have that. My neighborhood was one that was definitely upper class and I didn't need that type of negative attention there. He stood there for a second mugging Sherice before finally walking off in the direction of the security booth. I didn't even ask him where Big Boy's dumb ass was or go off on him like I wanted to because getting Sherice's nut ass off my property was more important.

"Why are you doing me like this, Elijah? You got these niggas out here manhandling me and treating me like a criminal! What? I'm not welcome here no more?" She turned her attention to me rolling her neck and talking all loud.

"Aye man, this bitch crazy." Trell mused looking around uncomfortably. Sherice was definitely out there doing the most and I wouldn't have been surprised if the police weren't on their way already. With mascara and smeared makeup covering her face, she looked like a mental patient as she set demented eyes on him.

"Nah, get yo lil ass outta here before I fuck you up Sherice!" I said through clenched teeth and snatched her back towards me. Her eyes widened fearfully and she took a step back, stumbling. I knew it was because of the dark look that took over my face. Sherice may not have been in the streets, but she knew me well enough to know when to stop pushing. I sighed irritably as she ran off and looked to my front door while Trell shook his head with a snort.

"Yooo she gone be a problem." He noted putting fire to a blunt I didn't even know he had. "You gone fuck around and have to kill her ass." I heard him talking, but I was hoping that shit wasn't true. As angry as I was the thought of killing her never crossed my mind, simply because I didn't handle females like that. I didn't have a problem dropping a nigga in the street, but women were a different story. If anything, I'd pay some hood rat to beat her ass, but I didn't even want it to go that far. That was until I saw my house. This whole time Big Boy had been inside trying to stop the water damage from this silly bitch stuffing all of my sinks and the tub and letting the water overflow. She'd also covered my walls and carpet downstairs with every condiment in my fridge. By the time Big Boy had made it to her, the damage was already done, and my floors and ceilings were fucked up. I stood in my living room fuming as water dripped from the ceiling and onto my furniture.

"Damnnn that bitch crazy for real! I hope you got insurance on this muhfucka." Trell quipped garnering a nasty scowl from me.

"Fuuuuuck!" I growled.

I was gone kill that bitch!

JUICE

"Aye, don't be touching my shit!" I snapped resisting the urge to pop this little nigga's hand. I wasn't in the mood to be babysitting especially when I didn't know this kid. The business we were in had me cautious about new faces, and the way this little nigga walked up on us was suspicious as fuck to me. Eazy could be all buddy-buddy with him, but I was gone keep my eyes open when he was around.

"Damn, my bad." He grumbled snatching his hand back quick as hell and flopping back into his seat. His little friend laughed in the back but quickly shut the fuck up with one look from me in the rearview mirror. I cut my music up and tried to press the gas harder so that I could drop their asses off faster. This shit was already taking time out of my day. I'd planned on diving into some pussy after our game, and now that shit was being postponed while I took some random ass kid's home. It didn't really matter because Makalah would wait, but it was the principal of this shit. Juice thought just because he was older than me that he knew better than I did about everything and that his word was law. He was lucky that I wasn't trying to bitch about some small shit like this or else I would've left these two little niggas right there at the Y. From the looks of them they were bad as hell and I could already tell that their mamas were some ratchet ass females that probably tricked niggas out of cash or stole shit just to keep them laced the way they were.

My face tightened at the thought. "Where the fuck you live man?" I questioned, hoping it wasn't too far away from where we already were. Without looking my way, he rattled off his address out in Calumet City, and it sounded familiar, but I paid it no mind until almost thirty minutes later when I was pulling up to the same duplex that Eazy and I had beat Dre's ass at.

"You live here?" I pointed up at the door with narrowed eyes.

"Yeah, so!" his tone was defensive and I immediately pulled out the gun I kept in my glove box, making his eyes widen in shock. Before I even took the safety off, he was shaking and shit, but I didn't give a fuck. I knew it was some funny shit going on when he brought his bad little ass in the Y and interrupted our damn game.

"Oh, you think you slick huh! Bring yall lil asses on!" I said tightly, nodding my head like everything was coming together for me, and in a way it was. We'd given Dre a week to come with our product or money, and since we hadn't come to collect right away, he thought he could send this kid to get some work for him. If he thought he was gone be able to pay us with our own shit then he had me fucked up! Now he was possibly about to catch a bullet this time because Eazy wasn't here to stop me! We didn't call that nigga Eazy for nothing, he was way more, easy going than I was because more often than not I was ready to shoot first and ask questions later. Since he was the reason I was in this mess in the first place, I would make sure he heard my damn mouth.

"Man, what the fuck you talkin bout?" Yo'Sahn had the nerve to be looking confused and shit as I climbed out and damn near yanked him out of the passenger side.

"That nigga Dre sent you to us? Huh!" I shook him as I asked.

Fear flashed across his face even though I never brought my gun up from my side.

"Nah man! I hate that nigga! I came because me and my mama need the extra bread. I swear, I already told Eazy!"

Before I could reply to him the sound of the screen door slamming into the house brought both of our attention to the porch where Dre was stomping down the stairs dragging a garbage bag behind him. I didn't even have to guess that it was full of his shit. I immediately released the little nigga with a shove and got ready to bring my wrath to Dre when the door came open again and shorty from the other day came rushing out with her arms full of loose clothes.

"Here take this shit with you too nigga!" she huffed tossing that shit over the banister and into the grass. She must have been chilling inside before this because all she had on was a black fitted t-shirt with the words boss bitch on the front and some black tights. Neither of them even noticed me as they continued to argue back and forth.

"Bitch! Don't touch my shit!"

"Why not, I paid for it! Nigga I'll throw this shit in the street, and I hope a car run over it!" she was pointing and rolling her neck as she snapped at him. Even though she was out here on some ratchet shit I couldn't help but admire how fine she was. She was a brown skin cutie and her body was sick as fuck. I could see her ass from the front and could tell that her waist was tiny as hell judging by the way her shirt fit. I didn't know if she was rocking a weave or one of them damn wigs that these hoes been going crazy over lately, but she had her hair pulled up into a ponytail that brushed the top of her ass, and swayed from side to side every time she spoke. *How the fuck this bum ass nigga get her?* I thought to myself and shook my head.

"Fuck you bitch! You talkin' all this shit like that lil Burger King job is somethin'! You just another bird like the rest of these hoes!"

"It's more than you and yo bird ass granny got bitch!" shorty shrugged, and Dre stopped picking up his clothes to try and run up on the porch. She didn't even flinch though, just threw her fists up like she was ready to throw down.

"Keep yo hands off my mama bitch!"

Yo'Sahn sped past me and up onto the porch with his little sidekick right behind him. Shit was looking like a whole WWE brawl and shit by the time I decided to break it up. I couldn't lie the shit had been mildly entertaining, but it wasn't what I'd signed up for and I didn't have time for it. Yanking up my sweats, I made my way over to the ball of bodies and pulled Dre away by his coat. This nigga wasn't wearing shit but a black coat with no shirt, and some black sweat pants. He was still swinging wildly, but I had a good foot on that nigga height wise, so he wasn't connecting with shit but my arms. The second he realized it was me though he calmed all the way down and his eyes bucked.

"Ju-Juice!"

"Yeah nigga Juice! Fuck our money at while you out here fighting females and kids and shit!" I growled holding him in the air while his feet dangled.

"I had it man on my granny, but this bitch's son took my shit out my pocket!"

"Bitch, don't lie on my baby!" Shorty came rushing over, but I gave her a look that had her stopping in her tracks.

"Nigga, I look like I'm tryna hear them sad ass excuses? You lucky y'all already got it hot out here or I'd decorate her yard with yo brains!" I threatened shaking his frail ass roughly. "You getting a pass today, but the next time I see you I'ma light yo hoe ass up!" The fact that I couldn't shoot his ass right then had me vexed, and it was like my body was vibrating I was so mad. I'd never liked Dre, he always gave me "fuck nigga" vibes, but one of the niggas that worked for us had vouched for him. Now I felt like I should kill his ass too, just for bringing Dre around! I tossed him to the side before I could change my mind about letting him go, and he got up and ran off so fast that he left all his shit lying in the yard. No longer concerned with him I turned my attention back to ole girl.

She watched him until his car disappeared around the corner while I got lost in her curves. "Excuse me, but me and my son ain't got shit to do with the money he owes yall, and I'd appreciate it if you didn't come back over here." She brought me out of my thoughts, snapping her fingers to get my attention. My eyebrows bunched together and I had to control the urge to call her ass a bitch.

"I just helped yo ass out twice! First, I brought yo bad ass son home and then I just stopped that nigga from stomping a mud hole in all y'all asses! You need to say thank you!"

"Brought my son home? From where? Why was he with you in the first place? Yo'Sahn get yo ass over here!" I groaned inwardly and contemplated just leaving her ass right there but decided against it. Even though I ain't like the little nigga he had heart, and I had to respect that shit. She yanked him forward as soon as he stopped beside her with a force that only a black mama could exhibit and asked him the same thing that she had asked me.

It may have been the look on his face, or the fact that I knew he was going to catch an ass whooping if she found out why he was with me, but I found myself speaking up on his behalf.

"Aye chill the fuck out, me and my brother got a mentoring thing going on. He came and signed up today, and instead of letting him ride the bus, I promised to bring him home. We ain't know he was you and dude son shit, we was just tryna help his lil ass out."

"That bitch ass nigga ain't my daddy!" Yo'Sahn protested, and his mama wasted no time popping him on the back of his head.

"Stop cursing!" she told him, before looking me over suspiciously. I didn't miss the appreciation that shone in her eyes when they landed on my dick, but I wasn't gone say shit. If she had been fucking with a nigga like Dre then she was probably long overdue for some "change yo life dick" I was sure of that. She ended her assessment with a raised brow, and I smirked already knowing what she was thinking about.

"How.....how do I know my son gone be safe with you? Just a couple weeks ago you and your brother were in my house pointing guns and making threats-."

"What you mean? I brought his lil ass here without a scratch on em!" I huffed cutting her off. "Look, we not tryna do shit but keep him outta trouble. He got my brother number, so if you want us to get him, he knows how to reach us. Fuckin with y'all I'm late for this pussy appointment."

I heard her gasp, but I ain't give her any time to respond before I was swaggering back to my damn car. I'd wasted enough time there already, and shorty wasn't even my problem. This was Eazy's little charity case, and he'd managed to suck me into it. I burned rubber pulling away from the curb, mad about a lot of shit, but mostly about how shorty was still on my mind.

By the time I got to Makalah's crib on the other side of town, I'd calmed down a lot. The two blunts I'd smoked on the way had helped, and I was hoping that after a shower and some good ass top I'd be ready to go and lay it down. Before I got out and faced that cold ass weather again, I texted and told her to come open the door, ignoring a call from Eazy as I waited. I already knew that he was gone be asking about little man and I wasn't trying to blow my high talking about that ghetto shit until after I'd busted a nut or two.

I saw her standing in the doorway and took my time shutting off my car and gathering my things trying to make sure I didn't leave shit before stepping out.

"Hurry yo ass up Juice!" Makalah hissed the second my damn Timb touched the pavement. I hadn't noticed that she'd brought her dumb ass to the door in only a robe until I made it to where she stood shivering in the hallway. She wasted no time slamming the door closed behind me and angrily strutting away making her juicy ass bounce underneath her sheer robe. I tossed my phone and keys on the couch once we entered the living room and snatched her up before she could go any further.

"Man, bring yo ass here." I cajoled lowering my voice as I pulled her thick body into mine. She tried to put up a small fight, but I knew she would stop once she felt my semi-hard dick up against her ass. If there wasn't nothing else that would put a stop to her attitude it was sex.

Makalah and I had been fucking around for almost six months, and she was a nice look. Shorty owned the condo she lived in and was an entrepreneur. She sold everything from weave, wigs, lashes, and them girly ass slides with fur on them. When we first hooked up, I let her know that I was dealing with a few other females and I wasn't trying to be on no exclusive shit. At the time she was down for it, but fast forward six months later, and she was demanding more and more from me. I couldn't really fault her, because she had that disease that most women had and that was thinking that she could change a nigga. No matter how many times I told her I didn't want a relationship, she was continuously asking or trying to force shit on me.

We'd just got into it last week because she wanted me to accompany her to some type of entrepreneur awards ceremony and I told her ass no. All she wanted to do was waltz me around pretending that we were a couple and then act a fool when I pressed up on one of the bitches there, proving that we weren't. I didn't even waste my energy trying to argue with her ass about it as soon as she started that loud shit I got the fuck out of dodge and today was the first time that I had been back since. Once she saw that I wasn't budging and was cool with not talking to her, she hit me up with that "I miss you" shit. As bad as I wanted to keep her on dick punishment, I had to admit that out of all the bitches I messed with she had the best pussy, and she was a freak out of this world. I'd fucked her in every hole but her ears, but I was sure if she thought I could she'd let me. For whatever reason though I couldn't wife her or any other woman for that matter. Where Eazy saw what our parents had and wanted to aspire to it, I didn't want to be tied down to one woman for the rest of my life, there were just too many options for that.

"Nah Juice." She moaned sexily. "What took you so long?"

I dodged the question by kissing on her neck, knowing that was her spot. A second later, she was in my arms with her legs wrapped tightly around my waist as I walked to her bedroom. After that whole scene I'd just left I wasn't trying to go back and forth with her, I just wanted to get my dick wet then go home. The quick shower that I'd taken at the Y was good enough for me to feel clean, but I needed my own custom made shower to get the tension out of my body. I wasn't prepared for Makalah's pussy to put my ass to sleep though. The last thing I remembered was the clock on her nightstand reading midnight, before closing my eyes.

DESTINY

"**W**elcome to Burger King, order when you're ready." I put on the most chipper voice that I could, but the truth was my feet were killing me, and I was ready to go home. Since Dream had been fired by that stupid ass boss of hers, we had to move up our plans, but it didn't hurt to continue to make money while we looked for a shop. I couldn't lie though I was excited as hell to be that much closer to our dream. It definitely helped me get through these long shifts a little bit better. My ass was in full hustle mode, and nobody could bring me down off my cloud.

"I'd like a whopper meal with cheese, no onions and a sprite." The deep baritone came through crystal clear, and a shudder ran down my spine. I already knew that voice well like I'd been hearing it for years, and I still wasn't sure why. After that whole fiasco with Dre in front of my house I'd only seen him once, and that was a week later when he brought Yo'Sahn's hardheaded ass home once again. That didn't stop me from lusting after his fine chocolate ass though. Forcing myself to calm down so as not to look thirsty I put in his order and told him to come around to the second window. Before his pearl white Escalade

35

pulled up, I already had a smile plastered on my face, but the second he rolled down his tinted window it disappeared.

Instantly I had an attitude at the sight of Makalah's thot ass in his passenger seat. She was an around the way hoe who stayed trying to bag a baller. We used to hang out in high school, and although we weren't besties or nothing, we were too close for her to have tried to fuck my baby daddy. I caught her texting his phone one day while he was in the bathroom and texted her back. From the long thread, it was clear that they had been talking for a minute or at the very least talking often. I had her meet me thinking it was him and beat her ass, then I went home and beat Antonio's ass too. It had been years, but she still left a nasty taste in my mouth, and I hated to see her coming. I slid the window open roughly and snatched the twenty-dollar bill out of his hand. He fixed his mouth into that cocky ass smirk he always gave me, but before he could speak I was closing my window on him. I could feel him grilling me as I got his change, but I kept my head down and finished at the register.

"Aye stop playin with me." He snapped grabbing my hand that I held out to him with his change.

"I don't know what you're talking about *sir*, but I'm going to need you to let me go so I can get your food." I managed to keep my tone even while my heart pounded rapidly. He studied me for a second with those serious brown eyes, before licking his lips and releasing me. Right away I felt the disconnect, but I didn't let it show as my coworker Ryan brought over his bag of food.

"Destiny-." He started but was immediately cut off by Makalah's thirsty ass.

"Destiny? Destiny Parker is that you? Hey girl!" The smile on her face was phony as hell just like the high-pitched enthusiastic tone she was using. "Antonio got you slavin' away at these people's restaurant? Couldn't be me." pity washed over her features, and I had to refrain from tossing Juice's food and drink on her dumb ass.

I chuckled bitterly and pointed a colorful acrylic nail her way. "Bitch don't play with me, I will drag your hoe ass all up and down this-!"

"Bitch?" she gasped, clutching her chest dramatically. "I got your bitch! Don't play with me and end up losing this lil job, bitch you know how I give it up!" Unmoved I watched her struggle with her seatbelt like she was about to do something, knowing this was all for show. I ain't want to get fired behind this messy bitch, but if she brought her ass anywhere near me, I was going to dog walk her.

"Makalah sit yo ass back, you know damn well you ain't bouta do shit, but get embarrassed!" Juice fussed instantly putting a stop to her weak attempt of getting buck.

She flung herself back against the seat with her arms folded like a little ass kid. "She started it though! You not gone say nothin to that bitch?"

"Nah you started it tryna be seen and shit! Don't let this lil ride go to your head shorty. I'll leave your ass right out here, and you still gone eat this dick when I call." Juice's face was balled up in irritation, and I was reminded of how fine he was when he was mad.

"Ahhhh and I oop!" I laughed loudly making sure to stick my tongue out at her.

"Calm that shit down, you out here letting bitches get you in yo bag and you got a shorty to feed! Give me my damn food and take yo ass back to work!" he got my ass right together. I sucked my teeth but did as he said, knowing that he was right. Makalah ain't have shit to lose, or shit to work for while I was out here doing it for Yo'Sahn. Embarrassed, I handed off his order and watched as he pulled off without another word. For some reason I felt like I had disappointed him, and it had me feeling some type of way. I had to quickly get over that shit though because my earphones were beeping indicating a car in the drive-thru.

* * *

I WAS FINALLY OFF, and I couldn't wait to get home and take a hot shower before bed. Yo'Sahn was at Jayden's house for the night, so I didn't have to worry about him. I was off the next day, and I planned to have a couple shots and sleep until further notice. It took me a half hour to get to my apartment, and once I got there, I wasted no time hurrying inside. The sun had already started going down, and my neighborhood wasn't the best, especially at a certain time of night. Even though I carried mace and a small pocket knife on me at all times, that was still no match for a gun, so I never took my time going from my car to my door.

As soon as I stepped inside, I flipped the switch, and the living room was bathed in light. The sight of a clean and quiet apartment felt good and reminded me of how much better things had been since I'd gotten rid of Dre's ass. I locked the door and set my things down on the end table before making my way to the back to prepare for my shower. After stripping down to only my thong, I went to cut on my water and waited a few minutes while it got hot enough for my liking. Then connected my phone to my beats pill speaker and had Kehlani station playing on Pandora. *"Worthy"* by Jeremih and Jhene Aiko came on, and I cut the volume all the way up, before going to pour me a couple of shots. The Patron quickly put me in a zone, and warmed my body as thoughts of Juice entered my mind. He probably didn't even realize that the way he'd handled me earlier was sexy as hell to me. That take charge, boss shit was everything to a bitch like me, especially after dealing with Dre's bum ass for so long.

I sang along to Kehlani's *"Night's like this"* as I washed my body with my Dove body wash. The hot water along with my loofa felt damn near like a massage to my sore muscles. I wished that I could sit in there for the rest of the night, but the way my hot water was set up, I couldn't take longer than fifteen minutes in the shower. I quickly washed three times and climbed out carefully since the Patron was starting to take effect. They ain't never lied when they said that shit snuck up on you. Wrapping a towel around myself, I headed to my room and sat at the foot of the bed to lather my body in coconut oil.

No sooner than I'd slipped into an over-sized t-shirt and climbed under my covers than loud banging at the door had me sitting up irritated. I wasn't expecting any company, so the intrusion wasn't welcome in the least, but since my baby wasn't home, I had to answer just in case it was him. Not bothering to cover up I stomped all the way to the door ready to go off especially if it was Yo'Sahn because he didn't have any business outside this time of night. I snatched the door open only to see Dre standing there. As irritated as I was, I couldn't lie he was looking good, but it might have been the alcohol talking. The cool night air had me pulling him inside instead of making him speak his peace on the porch like I should have. I closed the door but didn't bother locking it since he wasn't going to be staying long.

"What you want Dre?" my tone disguised how irritated I really was. The last time I'd seen him, he had gotten sonned, and was talking crazy. I couldn't even imagine what the fuck he could possibly have to say to me at this point.

"I came to holla at you, shit was outta control last time, and I feel like we need to talk before we just let all the years we've been together go." He shrugged as he stared down at me intently.

"You gotta be fuckin kidding me." I chuckled sarcastically. My response had his forehead creasing because this was usually the moment when I'd allow him the chance to beg his way back into my house and bed. That shit wasn't happening this time. I wasn't lying when I said I was done with him. He'd knowingly lied on my son to niggas that would've and could've killed him. I had forgiven Dre for many things, but this time he'd really fucked up.

"What you mean?"

"I mean, you're a damn joke, and you gotta be smoking bath salts if you think I'm letting you back in here around my son and me." I could already see the wheels in his head turning as he tried to think of a come-back that would work in this situation, but I wasn't trying to hear shit. Honestly, I shouldn't have even let his ass inside when I found him on my doorstep, but I was caught off guard and still buzzing. The dumb shit that had just come out of his mouth brought me back to reality though real fast.

"So, you takin his side again?" he questioned lamely, falling back on his same old mind games.

"You know what-! Bye Dre!

Ignoring the anger that flashed across his face, I headed towards the door and opened it back up so that he could make his exit. I was done with him and the conversation. What I wasn't expecting was for Juice to be standing on the other side looking like he was ready to murder us both, before shaking his head and walking off. Ignoring me as I called out to him, he swaggered to his car and screeched off into the night.

DREAM

Not waking up to Sherice's crazy demands every day felt good as hell! When I was working for her, my day started promptly at six in the morning. I had to wake up an hour early just so that I could get myself ready before she called me at seven with her list of shit she needed me to do. Of course, that was so that she could waltz her ass into the office right before lunch as if she didn't have a whole business to run. She'd ask for the work I'd gotten done in her absence and then wave me away to fetch her food and Starbucks. Most days I wouldn't even get my full hour because I spent the time running around for her, so I'd have to eat on the go.

Now I spent my mornings over a nice cup of tea and either reading or journaling. After that, I'd exercise then take a nice shower before looking at different properties for me and my sister's shop. So far, I wasn't having any luck in finding someone willing to work with us on our down payment. I'd unsuccessfully applied for numerous business loans and was denied every time for some reason or another, but I wasn't going to let that discourage me. The freedom I was feeling right now was intoxicating, and I didn't want to have to give that up by working for another person. I'd gotten some business by sharing some of my work on social media, but it was nowhere near enough to float me until we got consistent clientele.

Today I woke up on a mission to get things done. Before I even changed out of my pajamas I was on my laptop scouring properties, and I wasn't planning on logging off until I found us a location. As usual, there were plenty of salons on the market, yet they were all out of our price range and had very strict guidelines. I wasn't losing hope though, and not even twenty minutes later the clouds opened, and God smiled down on me. Whoever this Rachel person was must have literally just put her shop up, and it was perfect. Not only that, but she was willing to take payments with a generous down payment. Nervously, I dialed the number listed and waited as it rang, hoping that she would consider taking the ten thousand that we had. I hadn't realized that I was holding my breath until a sweet voice answered, and I released a deep sigh.

"Hello?" she jingled cheerily, yet confusion was evident in her tone. I wouldn't say that she was extremely old, but she sounded to be about in her late forties perhaps.

"Hi, this is Dream Parker, and I was calling to speak with Rachel about the salon for sale." I put on my most professional voice.

"Oh, oh wow! I just put the ad up not too long ago and already got two calls! E.J. I got another call!" Even though she sounded excited, my heart sank knowing that I hadn't reached her first. She didn't realize it but her shop was me and my sister's destiny, and I couldn't risk her giving it to someone else. As she talked to what I assumed was her husband in the background, I tried to think of an offer that would sway her. All me and Destiny really had was what we'd saved, and there was no one that we could call on to assist us. Our father had been in and out of our lives for as long as I could remember and our mother, well she had always been there, but hadn't always been there if you know what I mean. She'd found more fulfillment in a bottle of Paul Mason than she did in being a mama to us. We'd grown up rather early, basically having to take care of ourselves since she couldn't and wouldn't after losing our daddy. The shit must have hurt her deeply because she still used drinking as a coping mechanism. She hadn't done anything with her life at all and barely had a pot to piss in or a window to throw it out. After years of getting evicted and living without utilities when she'd decide that drinking was more important than keeping a roof over our heads and the lights on, she'd finally gotten it somewhat together, once we became adults. Still, I knew that I couldn't call her for this. Vicki didn't save money, so I knew damn well she wouldn't have a couple of thousand dollars and if she did, she damn sure wouldn't give that shit to us. She already had discouraged our business by claiming that everybody and they mama was doing hair and lashes right now. I knew that she was just jealous of us for taking a step in the direction of ownership when she'd wasted away over a man that wasn't thinking about her. I never let much of what she said effect anything that I had going on, but it still hurt to not have her support in anything.

My mind was still stuck on me and my mama's turbulent relationship when I heard her come back on the line sounding out of breath.

"I'm sorry about that." She chuckled. "This is just so exciting, you know I've been in the business for *years,* and it's finally time I go ahead and retire. My boys are both grown, and I just want to spend my golden years traveling and loving on my husband."

"Awww well congrats on your retirement it must be a wonderful feeling?" I found myself smiling as I talked because even though I didn't know her, I could tell she was a sweetheart with a bit of sass and I already liked her.

"Why thank you, it definitely is! Now the hard part will be actually letting go, but that's with anything you've poured so much into. As you can see from the pictures it's been well maintained, and I've even made a few upgrades….. you were going to be opening up a salon of your own right?"

"Oh yes, yes. We'll be opening up a hair and lash salon…if things go well."

"That's great! I can tell you're as passionate about your craft as I am and that's always a plus. If you have time, I can meet you later on today at the shop, and we can discuss this further."

"Later today?" I squawked completely caught off guard by how sudden it all seemed.

"Yes, today if you're available, if not I can-."

"No! I mean….today would be perfect, whatever time you can fit me in I'll be there." I didn't mean to sound so frantic, but there was no way that I could let the opportunity to get this salon pass me by. The fact that the price wasn't too steep and the place was absolutely gorgeous were both reasons enough for me to jump at it. Plus I already felt like Rachel, and I would get along great. The way she talked showed just how much she cared about her business, and I knew that if nobody else would give us a chance, she would.

"Okay, well how about 11:30? Is that alright?"

" Actually, 11:30 would be great. I'll see you then." I gushed, doing a good job of hiding the fact that I was kicking my legs excitedly.

"Okay sweetie, talk to you later." She said before hanging up.

Gleefully I hopped off the couch and started twerking to an imaginary beat in my head before looking at the time. I literally had two hours to get dressed, do my hair, and gather our paperwork. As I rushed to my bedroom to search for something fabulous to wear, I repeatedly dialed Destiny's number and kept getting the voicemail. I really wanted her to be there for this, especially if things went well, but I didn't have time to stalk her. Hopefully, I'd have all the time in the world once we got the keys.

An hour and a half later, I was showered and dressed in a black, skintight turtleneck with black and white checkered pants and some strappy black heels. It was cute and professional enough without looking overly dressed. With my natural hair in a high bun, I slipped on my rose gold Michael Kors watch and a simple cross necklace and glanced at myself in the mirror pleased with my look. After adding some red lipstick, I was out the door and on my way to my future.

I pulled up in front of the salon, formerly known as Rachel's and released a deep sigh. I'd managed to get there with five minutes to spare and I needed it to calm my racing heart. This would be the opportunity of a lifetime if things went right, and it would catapult me and my sister into entrepreneurship. After being denied right and left, I needed *something* to go in our favor.

Finally, after I'd gotten myself to calm down, I stepped out of my 2012 Mazda and sashayed to the glass double doors. Before I could knock a beautiful older lady that strongly resembled Phylicia Rashad came and swung it open with a huge smile. Her hair was long and thick, hanging down her back and she looked very angelic in her all-white blazer and pants suit.

"Hi, you must be Dream, beautiful name by the way. I'm Rachel King." I quickly accepted the hand she extended to me, calmed even more by the softness and warmth it held.

"Hello, it's so nice to meet you Mrs. King."

"Oh, please call me Rachel."

I simpered still shaking her hand profusely as she ushered me inside. When I finally did take my eyes off of her, I gasped in awe. The pictures on Trulia hadn't done this place justice at all. Hardwood floors that looked freshly waxed covered the room, with four white leather chairs lining each side. The stations all had huge rectangular mirrors in front and behind them were shelves to house each stylist's supplies. To the right of me was the receptionist desk and waiting area also filled with plush looking white leather chairs and a gigantic window that I hadn't noticed before in my nervousness.

"Well." She sighed with a smile after managing to remove her hand from mine. "It looks like you're already quite impressed with what you see so far, would you like a grand tour?"

Nodding wildly, I followed her through the shop as she showed me where everything was including the back where there were five wash basins and another room that would be perfect for doing lashes and brows. I could hardly contain my eagerness once the tour was finally over, and we sat down at the glass desk in the office to talk. I was still taking everything in and picturing me and Destiny coming here every day. The office alone was so big that we could both fit desks inside with room to spare. It was easy to get lost in the possibilities, but a small sense of fear still crept up and had me worried that this was out of our league. It just seemed too good to be true. As Rachel looked over our business plan and proposition, I anxiously waited for her to speak.

"This all looks wonderful and is very well put together Dream." She complimented, eventually lifting her gaze to mine. "It says here that you and your sister would be running things together?"

"Ahem. Ye-yes, she's working right now, so she wasn't able to come on such short notice." The lie tumbled out garnering a slight nod from her. Truthfully, I didn't have a clue where Destiny was, but I couldn't say that without the risk of sounding like we weren't serious about this.

"Okay well, I have to be honest honey. Ten thousand is a very low offer." She silenced my attempt at speaking with a raised hand, and my shoulders slumped in defeat. "Lucky for you, I have a soft spot for hard-working women, plus two sons and a husband that provide me a very comfortable life. So, here's what we can do. I'll take the ten and let you guys rent to own for say, fifteen hundred a month, with the condition that occasionally you let an old lady come through and work just to keep myself busy."

I blinked rapidly unsure of if I heard her correctly. "Re-really?" I gasped with tears stinging my eyes.

"Why not? I see a lot of myself in you Dream, and besides that, I feel like I can trust you to keep this place running. As long as you agree to the terms then we can get this show on the road."

"What! Hell yes I agree! Thank you, thanks so much!" The tears I'd been trying so hard to hold back were now running down my face as I ran around the desk and grabbed her up into a hug that I'm sure she wasn't expecting, but she obliged me anyway. She had a mother's touch and her hug was both comforting and reassuring.

Not too much later we were chatting like old friends and going over me and Destiny's ideas for the salon, all of which she seemed pleased and impressed by. It would only take a week or so to get our agreement drafted up and to get the sign changed, plus we had to meet with the four stylists to see if they would be staying on or if we'd need to hire more. We were in the middle of discussing this when the bell over the front door jingled, alerting us of someone entering.

"Aye ma! Ma where you at?" In the empty salon, the voice thundered echoing into the office where we sat.

"Oh there's one of my boys now!" Rachel swooned before making her way to the door. "We're back here Elijah!"

I also stood and prepared to meet the son of such a wonderful woman. No doubt he had to be just as awesome as she was. Smoothing the wrinkles from my clothes I had my head down making sure I looked presentable when he entered.

"Hey baby, I want you to meet Dream one of the new owners of the shop." I heard her say and looked up only to be stunned into silence.

"Well, looks like we meet again." He cheesed, eyeing me, and showing off all of his pearly-white teeth as he rubbed his hands together bird man style. Instantly my stomach dropped at the sight of the man who'd cost me my damn job. I honestly didn't know if I wanted to slap or hug him, but I couldn't help but to admire him from head to toe. Elijah looked as handsome as the day I met him even though he was dressed down in a red, Pelle Pelle leather coat, with a gray Nike pullover underneath, stonewashed jeans and some red timbs. Whatever cologne he wore filled the room and had me clenching my thighs shut tightly. Fighting my attraction, I tried to keep a hardened expression as Rachel looked back and forth between the two of us.

"You guys know each other?"

"Ummm-."

"Something like that, ma." He drawled sexily cutting me off. "Dream works for

Sherice-."

"Used to, I used to work for Sherice. Your little stunt got me fired." I couldn't help but roll my eyes as he chuckled like something was funny. His poor mother was stuck looking between us, baffled.

"She fired you for that?" He huffed like it was no big deal and pulled his phone out. "I'll call her ass right now and-."

"No need. As you can see, I'm going to be taking over your mother's salon." I told him smugly unable to stop the wide grin I felt spreading from being able to say that. Elijah's brows lifted, impressed, and he looked to his mother to confirm.

"Oh, well I guess that means I did you a favor.....so I'll accept dinner as a thank you." My mouth dropped as he smirked and straightened his jacket. I was more than surprised because honestly, I thought that he'd only said he wanted me to have his number to piss Sherice off that day. That could very well still be the case though, so despite the obvious attraction I felt towards him, I wasn't about to be a part of his and Sherice's little game.

"Excuse me,"

"Since getting fired ultimately resulted in you opening up your own business, I think you should have dinner with me. It's the least you could do really." He shrugged clearly enjoying the irritation he was causing me.

"Boy-."

"Okay, so it's settled then. I'll pick you up tonight at about eight." Before I could object, he turned to give Ms. Rachel a kiss and was out the door. The cocky manner in which he'd just handled me was......sexy as hell, and something I wasn't used to. I had to admit that I liked it. As I stood there still lusting after him, Ms. Rachel turned my way with a knowing look of her own.

"Why don't we finish up here, so you can go and get ready for your date." I didn't miss the amusement in her voice as she took her seat back at the desk. If she and her son thought that I was going anywhere with him, they were sadly mistaken, but I wouldn't tell her that now. I had more important things to do with my Friday night than to spend it with him. We were opening up a business, and I didn't need the distraction of any man, let alone Elijah King.

JUICE

 $\mathcal{I}$ laid back against Makalah's array of pillows and watched my dick disappear down her throat, as thoughts of Destiny filled my head. It had been a minute since I went over there with the intentions of apologizing, except the sight of Dre had me looking at her funny. As bad as I wanted to go upside that nigga's head, I wasn't trying to do that shit where her and Yo'Sahn lived, and I also didn't want her thinking it was over her. Seeing that nigga in her crib while she was dressed in only a t-shirt definitely had me feeling some type of way, but I'd never let a bitch know she had got to me. From the look on her face, she knew she had fucked up too and tried to stop me from leaving, but it was too late. As far as I was concerned, she could have that dusty ass nigga, as long as he paid me my money. Because if he didn't bring me what he owed, then she'd be burying his ass.

"What the fuck Juice, you can't keep a hard dick with me now?" Makalah's whiny ass voice interrupted my thoughts. When I focused in on her, she was looking up at me with a scowl, as she held my semi-erect dick in her small hand.

"If you'd do the shit right maybe it would be." I snapped irritably. The truth was that with Destiny so heavy on my mind, I couldn't focus on shit else. Offended, she stood up making her ass and breasts jiggle in the process.

"You got me fucked up now, you know my mouth game vicious. Don't try and play me!" she scoffed. Even though the situation didn't call for it, I couldn't contain the chuckle that escaped me. This bird-brained bitch was bragging about her throat skills and not even realizing that she was turning me off even more. "What the fuck is funny, nigga?"

"Yo ass."

"What?" her voice got increasingly more aggressive as I stood and began to redress. I wasn't about to do this goofy ass shit with her not today or any other day. This was one of the main reasons why I wasn't trying to wife a bitch. Not only was she ratchet as fuck, but she didn't even think that maybe I had some shit on my mind that was affecting my erection. She probably didn't give a fuck, because from my experience all these hoes only cared about how much money a nigga had, and how big his dick was. Regardless of me not wanting to be serious with her, she was willing to take whatever I could give her just to be able to say that I fucked with her on occasion.

I ignored her staring me down as I pulled on my briefs and black Gucci jeans.

"Where is you going? I'm still talking to you!" She moved to stand in front of me, not bothering to cover up as she hollered.

"Calm that shit down Kay!" I growled after snatching up my shirt and hoodie. Arguing with bitches was something that I didn't do, and her jumping around in my face was the fastest way to get hemmed up. Silently, she moved across the room, but she continued to glower my way, only speaking again when the space between us had grown.

"You got me so fucked up! You know how many niggas want me? I'm turning down niggas every day trying to stick by you so that you see I'm down for yo ass, and you can't even get hard when I'm sucking yo lil ass dick!"

By now she was pacing the floor as she ranted, while I slipped my feet into the Jordan 13 retros I'd worn. She wanted me to argue back with her ass so bad that she was trying to lie on a nigga. Makalah knew damn well wasn't shit little on me, especially not my dick.

"Yeah, ayite." I tossed out over my shoulder and made my way out of the room, with her following closely behind me. She'd done all that talking, and all it was doing was pushing me to drop her ass off my roster. Makalah knew she wasn't my only one, she had just been my favorite for a while, but the more she talked, the less I was feeling her.

I allowed her to keep on with that rah-rah shit as she stomped after me going off about other bitches and some more shit. When I reached her front door, she realized that I wasn't playing and did some ninja shit that landed her in front of me and against the door blocking my exit.

"Why you leaving? I'm sorry for what I said just don't go...I-, I can try something different." She begged her tone suddenly turning soft and whiny. Unmoved I pried her fingers from my hoodie and firmly pushed her aside.

"Nah, I'm good." It was obvious that sex was out of the question for the night and if we weren't fucking, then there was no reason for me to be in her presence, especially after all of the shit she'd been talking. I slammed the door behind me hoping that she wouldn't bring her dumb ass outside acting a fool and made my way to my new matte black, Audi. Even though the block was fairly busy with bitches trying to be seen and niggas out there fucking off, I wasn't at all worried about leaving my shit out there. Everybody knew not to touch anything that belonged to us from the south side to the west. Eazy and I had come up majorly in the dope game, and it had garnered us respect and fear. If you didn't work for us, then you wanted to, and that counted for the whole city.

I nodded to the few niggas that were out who deserved a greeting and ignored the others that weren't about shit while glancing briefly at a few of the neighborhood thots that were out. The cold hadn't stopped shit out this way. I guess living here you got used to the unpredictable weather. As soon as I sat my ass in the plush leather seat, my phone started vibrating in my pocket. Frowning at Yo'Sahn's name, I slid the bar across the screen and waited for him to come on the line.

"Hey Juice!"

"What's up lil man?" I questioned reclining my seat back. As much as I'd been against his little ass being around in the beginning, I couldn't deny that he'd grown on me. It was mostly due to how much heart he'd displayed helping his mama when that fuck nigga Dre was out there trying to clown on her. While she hadn't agreed to letting him spend time with me and Eazy his bad ass hadn't listened and had been kicking it at the boys and girls club that Eazy often volunteered at. I'd been around a few times when my brother called himself hanging out with little man, and I had to admit that he wasn't so bad. Yo'Sahn had my number as well as Eazy's and was under strict instructions to call us for whatever.

"Can you come get me- aye don't touch me man!" I could hear him scuffling with someone in the background and sat up frantically, starting my car and putting it in gear.

"Yo'Sahn! Yo'Sahn, where you at?" I yelled loudly hoping that he could hear me since it was clear that he was no longer holding his phone. Beeping indicated that the call had dropped stopping my futile attempts. I sped off while thumbing Eazy's number in only to be met by his voicemail. Angrily I punched the steering wheel not knowing exactly what was going on and getting pissed off. Too much shit was going on in these streets for Yo'Sahn to be out here alone. Anything could be happening to him, and I didn't even know where to start looking. That didn't stop me from driving furiously towards his house, with my eyes peeled for him. My phone rang in my hand and I answered without looking.

"Yo-."

"Aye bossman," I wasn't expecting for it to be Grim on the other line when I answered and my brows furrowed in irritation.

"What man!" I said through gritted teeth not wanting to be bothered, but knowing that if he was calling, then it was important.

"These lil out west niggas trippin, they got two shorties out there in front of the crib, tryna make an example out they lil asses." He informed, sounding like he was out of breath. Instantly I froze. There was no way he could be talking about Yo'Sahn and his little homie.

"How they look?" I questioned busting a U-turn in the middle of Michigan and not giving a single fuck about the horns blaring in response.

"Shit short, one light-skinned and the other one dark-skinned. Neither one of them look no older than 14 though. Oh yeah, they both got some lil ass dreads." He added as an afterthought. Even though half the kids in Chicago had dreads and were out here being bad as hell, I felt it that he was talking about Yo'Sahn and his homie.

"Oh shit! They just dropped the dark-skinned one on his head!"

"Aye, line them niggas up right now, don't let them do shit else, I'm on my way!" I hung up before he could object and sped up, making the half hour trip to the west side in less than fifteen minutes. When I pulled up I saw Grim standing in front of a group of about five niggas on our payroll, while Yo'Sahn and his friend stood off to the side nursing a busted head and a fat lip. I grabbed my gun out of the glove box and instead of tucking it into my jeans like I normally would I held it tightly in my right hand as I got out, barely putting the car in park.

When Yo'Sahn saw me his eyes widened, seeing that I was carrying a gun, and he tried to say something, but I ignored it as I came to a stop in front of our crew. He knew he didn't have any business out here like this and he was really lucky that all he'd gotten was a busted lip.

"Which one put they hands on you?" I asked over my shoulder as I looked them each in the face. All at once they began to plead their cases, but I wasn't trying to hear shit. Even if they had a valid reason for what they'd done, which I was sure that they didn't the fact still remained that while they were out here harassing little ass kids, money was not being made. I felt Yo'Sahn next to me before I saw him, and waited while he looked at each one trying to figure out who it was that had fucked him up. His face was bright red from fighting, and he was still panting letting me know that the shit had just been broken up.

"This nigga!" He spat pointing out Savion, before wiping a small bit of blood from his lip. Frowning I stepped closer, and before I could even say shit, he was explaining.

"Man fuck that! These lil muhfuckas called themselves tryna steal up out the trap!" Savion kept his angry glare on Yo'Sahn, but regardless of what he told me shorty wasn't the one under fire. It actually made them look worse to me that they'd allowed their young asses inside of my fucking spot like that shit was cool. I glanced Yo'Sahn's way and could tell from the look on his face that there was some truth to what dude was saying, but I wouldn't address it right then.

"We ain't do shit!" Jayden shouted running over and making an attempt to fight Savion. I grabbed his little ass back by the hood of his jacket and held him in place by my side. He was Yo'Sahn's right hand, but I couldn't help but feel like he was always pushing him into bad shit.

"Aye calm yo lil ass down!" I gritted and gave him a shake to stop him from struggling. "Now tell me who the fuck did that shit to yo head." His face was balled up in rage, and I could already tell from the murderous gleam in his eyes that he was going to grow up to be a problem. I'd seen that look on countless faces, and it held no hope. For sure he would be one of the many statistics out here if he didn't wring that shit in. Instead of pointing, he jutted his chin in Savion and Gin's direction.

Shaking my head in mock disbelief, I stepped closer and lifted my gun until it was right in Savion's face. "You sure it was this nigga? Cause it ain't no way the muhfuckas I'm paying is out here making the block hot with some petty ass bullshit! Right, Savion? You ain't really do no shit like that?" Fear filled his eyes as I scrutinized him closely, but he kept his chin up, so he didn't look like a bitch.

"N-naw man-."

"So they lyin? And my nigga Grim over here lyin too huh?" It was a rhetorical question, but he still tried to say something, and I snuffed his ass midsentence. "I don't give a fuck nigga! You grown as hell out here in the streets fightin' two lil ass kids! In front of my shit!" I continued to hit him until he was curled up on the ground with blood pouring from his mouth as everybody stood by and watched. Next was Gin. Lucky for him I was too tired to deliver the same ass whooping that Savion got, but after two uppercuts to the chin, he dropped like a bag of rocks right next to his boy. Out of breath, I stood over the two with my gun on them as I addressed the group. "Let this be a warning to all y'all niggas! Y'all see these two, right here? Next time y'all see them around don't even sneeze in their direction, and that goes for everybody around this bitch! Do I make myself clear!"

A chorus of "yeahs and you got it" sounded and I scanned the crowd for Grim, spotting him in the back still standing next to his car, with an uneasy look on his face. I gave him a slight nod, and he already knew what I wanted. It was already too much going on out there and plenty of witnesses to my assault. I wasn't stupid enough to get my hands dirty with so many witnesses around. I didn't care how many people we had on the payroll or who feared us. You wouldn't catch me doing some shit that would get me jammed up.

After getting confirmation from him that both Gin and Savion were going to be taken care of, I shut the house down for the rest of the night and ordered Yo'Sahn and Jayden into my car. The smile on Jayden's face was hard to miss, and he talked excitedly, even while he had a big ass knot forming on his head. Yo'Sahn, on the other hand, was quiet, obviously mulling over the day's events.

"Man you that nigga for real! I wish you would've let me get a hit in on they ass! That shit was just lit!"

I narrowed my eyes at him through the rearview, wanting to knock him upside the head. "Nah, that shit was stupid! My niggas are trained to go, and that shit could've gone a completely different way. Ain't no telling what could've happened to y'all if Grim hadn't told me where y'all was at!" This little nigga wasn't trying to hear shit I was saying and had his face frowned up as I spoke.

"Mannnn."

"Ain't no man muhfucka! You think you built for this shit? You focused on the wrong shit my nigga. Take yo lil ass to school and chase behind some fast ass lil girls, stay out the fuckin streets! This ain't for you!" I barked angrily just as I pulled up in front of his house. Everything I'd said had gone in one ear and out the other, but at least I tried. I know me and my brother's lifestyles seemed glamorous to them, and as much as I loved the money and the things that came with it, I didn't want that shit for either of them. I watched as he nodded while reluctantly grumbling an okay, and dapped up Yo'Sahn before hopping out of the car. The car was silent with Jayden gone, and it remained that way until my car came to a stop at Yo'Sahn's house. I could damn near hear his heart beating as he looked up at the door anticipating his mama's reaction, and I almost wanted to laugh at his bad little ass. If I couldn't say shit else about Destiny, it was that she went hard for her son and would get in his ass when need be. Him coming home with a busted lip was going to for sure activate her wrath.

"Don't get scared now big man." I half-joked as I took the keys out and climbed from the car with mixed feelings about seeing his mama again. I was already on the porch and had rung the bell by the time he finally stepped out himself. As he made the short walk up the steps, the door opened up, and Destiny stood on the other side looking confused and then irate when she saw his face.

"What the hell! What happened to your face!" she swung the door the rest of the way open and yanked him inside, gripping him by his cheeks and examining his face with furrowed brows.

"It's nothin ma-."

"Don't tell me it's nothin when you sporting a fat lip!" she shrieked cutting him off.

"Look, I don't know what happened exactly, by the time I got there he was already fucked up." I shrugged while she continued to check him out. Upon my revelation, she brought her weary eyes my way.

"I guess I should say thank you, it could have been way worse than just him getting beat up."

"Man, I ain't get beat up." Yo'Sahn finally spoke, with his face balled up. I swear you would have sworn that he'd slapped her the way her head reared back.

"I know you better get your smart mouth ass in your room before I fuck you up!" she snapped starting in his direction, but I gripped her arm lightly and stopped her, while he made his get away.

"Get in his ass later, I gotta holla at you about something real quick." Confusion showed on her face, but she didn't fight against me like I was expecting her to.

"About?"

"About Yo'Sahn." With a nod, she followed me into the small kitchen where we stopped beside the stove. "I think you need to watch him around Jayden's lil ass. I don't really like that lil nigga like that and the more they kick it, the more trouble Yo'Sahn gets in."

"What? No, Jayden's a good kid." She tried to say, but I shook my head firmly.

"Nah, keep his ass away from Yo'Sahn or he gone stay in trouble." I told her despite her denial. I planned on having this conversation with Yo'Sahn too just at a later time, but I was serious about him not being around that little nigga.

"Okay, well, can we talk about the other night?" she asked hopefully.

"Ain't shit to talk about, my only interest is your son you can keep that other shit." She seemed stunned by my reply, but it was the truth. Even though I was feeling some type of way about seeing her ex around, I'd never let her know it. Without giving her a chance to say shit else, I mumbled a goodbye and dipped while my mind ran wild with thoughts of Destiny.

EAZY

*I*t was ten minutes until I was due to pick Dream up when I pulled into her driveway. I smirked when I saw the curtains move, indicating her presence in the window. She could pretend all she wanted, but I knew that she wanted me.

I stepped out of my Rolls Royce, Cullinan and smoothed a hand down the front of the maroon sweater I was wearing. Even though I had business to attend to after leaving the shop earlier, I'd made sure to have it all finished so that I would be on time. So far, things had been running fairly smooth with the exception of a couple of incidents. I was always the type to handle things before they got out of control or before there was anything to handle. That was one of the main reasons why shit had gone so well for us, besides the fact that Juice and I never hesitated to bust our guns. In addition to taking care of our business dealings, I'd also gathered as much info on Dream as I could on such short notice. She was beautiful and educated, but Sherice had been too and look how that shit turned out. Nothing came up on her, but I guess being a sneaky, lying ass hoe wouldn't pop up on somebody's background check, so I was going out on a limb and assuming the best.

Ringing the bell, I could hear shuffling behind the door, before a long silent pause, that had me shaking my head. "Open the door Dream, I already know you're in there." I couldn't believe that she had me out there sounding like a damn stalker, but I wasn't going to leave without her fine ass.

"How do you know where I live?" she questioned suspiciously from the other side of the door. I coughed to hide the chuckle that came out because she obviously didn't know who I was. Even if I hadn't been able to get her information on my own, she'd still filled out some paperwork with my mama earlier that day. I could have just as easily gotten them from her because unsurprisingly my mama loved Dream and was on board with me pursuing her.

"Does that really matter, I'm already here, just open the door."

"How do I know you're not some damn crazy person, popping up over here like this?" came next and this time I couldn't control my laughter. Shaking my head once more, I ran a hand over my waves. I knew that she was only stalling, and it was kind of cute.

"Dream, you know I'm not crazy, if I were then I would have already found a way in without alerting you that I was out here. Now it's cold as hell, you gone make me sit out here getting sick or you gone let me in?"

A second later the locks turned, and she pulled the door open to reveal her looking like a model even though she was completely dressed down in an oversized, gray biggie sweatshirt and some black leggings. Her pretty toes were on display in some furry, black UGG slides, and I had to admit that the white polish had me ready to put them in my mouth. I licked my lips as my eyes traveled back up her body slowly to be met with an irritated expression. Dream was giving me Brook Valentine vibes, with her attitude and looks alone.

"So, you gone put on some shoes so we can go?" I asked easing inside of the small hallway, forcing her to back up so that I could close the door behind me. Her breath caught in her throat from our close proximity, and I grinned. *Yeah, she was definitely feeling the kid.* I thought as I further invaded her space.

"I-ahem! I don't remember agreeing to go anywhere with you." Her brows bunched, but the lust in her eyes was evident.

"Dream, why you making this so difficult woman? You know you want to come with me, so stop all this extra shit and go get your shoes." Shocked, her eyes widened from my tone, but as fine as I thought she was I wasn't about to keep sitting here damn near begging her to leave with me. On a good day, I was turning women away left and right, but she was making me jump through all of these hoops just for a dinner date. I was just about ready to get the fuck on when she finally uncrossed her arms and let out a sigh.

"Well, I can't go nowhere if you don't let me out of this corner." She huffed. Giving her a wide grin, I stepped back and allowed her the room to go and get herself ready while I took the opportunity to look around. Her house smelled fruity, with a small hint of cleaning products which let me know that she had recently cleaned up, and her living room further proved it. The space was small so all that fit inside was a small royal blue, suede love seat, a coffee table, and a flat-screen. The entire room was decorated in all white and royal blue, which was my favorite color, so that was another plus in my book. Nothing was out of place in there, and that told me that she was a neat freak. Even the fashion magazines that lined her coffee table were placed perfectly. I nodded my head in approval and took a seat on the couch, before pulling out my phone and checking my messages. There were a few missed calls from Juice, but he hadn't left a voicemail, so I wasn't going to sweat it at the moment. I was in the middle of deleting emails when the sound of heels clacking, entered the room and drew my eyes Dream's way.

She'd gone back and changed into a skintight, black dress with long lacy sleeves and some thigh high boots that only left a sliver of brown skin visible. Her hair was slicked back into a ponytail that hung down past her ass. I adjusted my dick discreetly and stood up, meeting her.

"Damn, you tryna kill me ma," I muttered unable to take my eyes off of her. Dream blushed but quickly tried to hide it by turning to the closet next to her hallway to grab her coat which gave me the perfect view of her round ass. I already imagined how it would look bent over while I gave her deep back shots when she spun around to face me again.

"Ready?" she smirked, probably knowing damn well what she was doing to a nigga in that short shit.

"Yeah, let's go."

"THIS WHERE WE EATING?" she seemed shocked when we pulled into the parking lot of Harold's Chicken. I brushed my hand down my face to hide my grin. Even though Dream didn't seem like the money hungry kind, I still had to make sure that she'd be down for a simple meal. Call me crazy, but I couldn't fuck with a female that couldn't get down on some chicken, or catfish with mild sauce. Sherice would occasionally eat it, but I could always tell that she was only doing it for my benefit and not because she actually liked it. There had always been a lot of signs telling me that she wasn't the one for me, and I'd over-looked them because she had a good head on her shoulders. I wasn't doing that shit anymore though, I was trying to look beyond the outward appearance from now on.

"Yeah, you like Harold's don't you?"

"Hell yeah, I'm just a little surprised." She shrugged.

"Surprised?"

"You just seem like the type that loves to throw money around to impress the women you date." She eyed me with humor on her face.

"Nah, I don't throw money around to impress nobody, but if I'm in love with a woman, then I'll spoil her rotten with anything her heart desires."

With that, I exited the car and came around opening the door for her with my hand out to help her onto her feet. I didn't let her pull away as I started towards the door where a small group of people stood.

"Aye man they saying they closed." One of them angrily grunted as we passed.

"Good lookin'." I tossed out, never breaking my stride. I was well aware that they were closed, to the public anyway.

"Wait, did he say they were closed?" Dream asked from beside me, still allowing me to guide her to the door where the manager stood waiting to let us inside.

"I got it all ready for you Eazy." She gushed garnering a look from Dream. Still, with her hand in mine, we followed her to the back where she had a table set up for us with a candle in the middle and a few surrounding the area we'd be dining in. I pulled out the chair for Dream, and she took a seat with a shake of her head.

"You rented out the Harold's," she chuckled as I sat down across from her. "You ghetto as hell." The smile on her face gave me reason to believe that despite her words, she wasn't mad about our little set up.

"Only the best. I gotta make sure you don't be trying to eat your chicken with a fork or no shit before I can decide if you're the one." She rolled her eyes and giggled.

"Naw, ain't no fork, I gets down and dirty with mine." Her eyes gleamed with the double meaning, and my eyebrows rose, "not like that!" she followed up quickly with her lying ass. It was cool though, even as conservative as she seemed I could tell that she had a whole lot of freak in her.

"Yeah, so you say." I teased. Just as she went to speak the manager, Mary returned with two menus and placed them on the table, with a bottle of Dom Perignon in a bucket of ice and two glasses that I'd had brought over earlier.

"Okay yall look over the menu, and I'll be back in a second." Mary said sweetly before waltzing away. I'd known her since I was a little nigga going to CVS and would stop through here on my way home from school. She was like a mother to Juice and me and the extra money I'd thrown her to close down for the night had been more than worth it.

"Dom?" Dream simpered lifting the bottle out of the ice. "I thought this was supposed to be something slight?"

"I don't care what I'm eating, Dom gone always be the drink of choice, besides, I need something good to help you relax and open up a little."

"You ain't tryna get me drunk so you can take advantage of me....are you?" a smile played at her lips as she poured us both a glass and slid mine across the table to me.

"Yo, you funny as hell man. Trust me though, I ain't gone have to get you drunk to get you in my bed, shit you already marinating for a nigga and I haven't even done shit yet." I smirked.

"Cocky much?"

"Not cocky, *confident* and with good reason."

She was saved from having to make a rebuttal by Mary appearing on the side of us, but I didn't miss the look of relief on her face. "Y'all ready to order?"

"Yep!" Dream said abruptly. "Let me get the six, piece wings with fries and mild sauce." Her voice had taken on a high-pitched tone, and her cheeks were flushed. I would bet my last dollar that the panties she had on were soaked. The thought had me licking my lips as I eyed her and ordered the same thing she had, sending Mary back to the kitchen.

Silence fell over the table as she drained her glass and tried to get herself together. I watched as she poured another and began to drink while I was still sipping from my first one. "So, you gone tell me something about yourself, besides what I don't already know?" I asked quietly.

Dream bashfully brushed her ponytail over her shoulder and shrugged. "Well, it isn't a whole lot to tell. I'm 27, no kids, but I have a nephew that's almost like my son." She smiled at the mention of him. "About to open up this salon with my lil sister and make a name for ourselves."

"Damn, no man included in those plans?"

"Why does there have to be a man involved? I'm trying to focus on coming up right now. These niggas don't want nothin serious anyway, and I'm much more than somebody's booty call." Her lip curled, and I detected a hint of bitterness. It was clear that she had been burned by some dumb ass nigga in the past and I wished that I could find whoever he was and beat his ass for her.

I sat back as Mary approached with our food so that she could sit the trays down in front of us, enjoying the smell. I had tasted all kinds of different, expensive foods since coming up, but it didn't have nothing on the simple restaurant food I'd grown up on. Mary set the food down and smiled graciously at our gratitude, before disappearing again to give us privacy.

"So you're not interested in love….marriage…kids?" I got back to my interrogation once Mary was no longer in sight, and chewed on a forkful of fries drenched in mild sauce while Dream thought over the question.

"I mean….eventually. What woman doesn't want all those things? I just think that I'm not ready to receive all that just yet. Enough about me though, tell me something about you *Eazy*."

She changed the subject quickly, and I decided to allow her a break, even though I wanted to hear more about her.

"Shiit, I'm 29, and single, as you know. No kids although I would love to have them one day. Despite other niggas my age I'm ready for a family and the whole nine." I paused as she unintentionally made my dick jump from the way she was sucking the mild sauce off of her fingers. "Ahem! I uh, I've got a few businesses, and I'm in the process of starting a mentorship program for some of the young boys out here. You know just to keep them off the streets, and shit." Keeping my illegal activities out of the conversation was a must at this point. Not only because I didn't know if I could trust her, but because she didn't seem like she'd be enthused about it.

"Really? That's actually cool as hell. I might have to tell my sister about it to keep Yoshi's lil bad ass out of trouble." Her eyes gleamed, and I felt pride in the fact that she approved of what I was trying to do.

"Yeah make sure you do that. Right now I only have one kid that I take to do lil shit, but I would love to be able to reach more." After that first meeting with Yo'Sahn, I had made sure to look out for him and keep him out of trouble, as much as I could. I'd even been able to get Juice's mean ass to stop being so hard on him, and now he was like a little brother that we had to tote around.

"That's what's up, it's not too many men out here looking out for these lil fatherless kids." She commended, with a genuine smile.

We continued to talk and get to know each other even after our food and the bottle was gone. I barely had a buzz, but it was obvious that Dream was good and tipsy as I helped her out of her seat and held her coat so that she could slip it back on. She was giggly as fuck and kept finding a reason to touch either my chest or face. Normally, I didn't like anybody putting their hands in my face besides my mama, but any type of physical contact I could get from Dream I wanted. She had me out here like a love-struck simp, and I hadn't even fucked her yet.

When we got back to my car, I helped her inside and went around to hop behind the wheel. Like a typical weekend, there was still plenty of people around even though it was well after midnight. Some were standing at a safe distance checking out my whip, but they all knew who it belonged to so nobody dared get too close. Pulling away from the curb, I took a quick glance in Dream's direction since she had gone silent and realized that she already had her eyes closed.

"You tired?" I scoffed in disbelief making her lips turn up at the corners, never opening her eyes.

"Hmmm, no," she mumbled the lie smoothly but shifted in the seat to make herself more comfortable letting her head drop to the side. Her ass was definitely out for the count. After the day she'd had, plus the drinks I could only imagine how tired she was. I gave myself a second to admire how fine she was as I turned up the volume on the Tory Lanes album that was playing and continued on to her crib.

"Aye Dream, wake up." I shook her gently once I came to a stop. She let out this moan that sounded sexy as hell and stretched before opening her eyes slowly.

"Damn, did I fall asleep?" She asked with an apologetic look on her face.

"It's cool, next time I know not to give yo ass any liquor." I teased.

"I can hold my alcohol, thank you."

I didn't reply just smirked as I got out, pleased that she hadn't immediately denied me a second date. I held the door and helped her out of the car enclosing her small hand in mine just like before and walked the short distance to her door with her at my side.

"Soooo, should I assume that you got my number when you

got my address?" She asked, looking up at me with her head tilted once we stopped on the porch.

"Something like that." I shrugged and stepped closer so that our chests were touching. "You saying that you want me to call you then?"

"Hmmm, I guess." She beamed playfully.

"Good, cause I was gone call yo ass anyway." Her head fell back as she laughed, and I fought the urge to plant a kiss on her slender neck. She was already tipsy, and I was feeling good myself, so I already knew where that would lead. I was trying to take things slow with her even though I was positive that she was my future.

"So fuckin cocky." She mused shaking her head. The movement brought her closer, and I couldn't resist placing my lips on hers. Eyes closed she allowed my tongue to explore her mouth, emitting a whimper as her body slumped against mine. I had a handful of Dream's ass, and it felt just as soft as it looked, making my dick swell against my jeans. If she hadn't pulled away a second later, I'm sure we would've been inside fucking soon.

"Th-thanks for dinner." Dream stuttered barely able to make eye contact. Her hands were shaking nervously as she fumbled with her keys. Holding back a laugh, I smoothly took them and opened her door for her, only leaving a small amount of room for her to squeeze by. I couldn't lie I enjoyed the effect I had on her. She tried so hard to act like she wasn't fucking with me like that, but her body language spoke volumes.

Once she slid past me working hard not to let her body touch mine, she seemed to relax. "You're welcome beautiful. Gone head and lock up." I told her and stood there until she'd done so before heading back to my car. It went without saying that I would definitely be seeing Dream again.

DESTINY

"*S*o you said she got two sons, right?" I asked my sister as we drove to meet with Rachel to go over some final paperwork. I'd already seen the shop and was immediately impressed, but if I were being honest, I wouldn't have cared what it looked like as long as I was able to make money in there. Dream and I both had a passion for hair, but I had only recently gotten into doing lashes and brows. It didn't take me long to become obsessed and I went and took a course so that I could get even better. All things that had to do with beauty were interesting to me, and now we could make a living from it. I'd already blocked both the numbers to my old jobs because I had no intentions on going back now that we'd found a location for our business. *Fuck em!*

Dream grinned at me and shook her head, but I was dead ass serious. She'd just finished telling me about her date, and I can't even lie I was jealous. I'd just gotten out of my situation with Dre and didn't have any business trying to talk to nobody else. Still, the nigga was driving a Cullinan, so he obviously had money and money was the biggest problem in my relationship. Well, lack of money, but you know what I mean.

"Bitch she does have two sons, but that doesn't mean he's anything like his brother. Besides, we only had one date, I still don't know him like that. He could be a straight asshole or a stalker. Shit, he could beat bitches." She said pointedly.

"You really need to stop watching all them crime shows, yo ass paranoid as hell." I sucked my teeth irritably. "Keep on with that *Snapped* shit and you gone end up old and alone." I was only teasing, but some truth rang in what I'd said. Dream had been single for a few years since her ex had caught a drug charge and got sentenced to a five-year bid. I always assumed that she was waiting on him and that was why she hadn't been dating anybody the whole time he'd been gone, but it was about time that she got the cobwebs knocked off her pussy. From what she'd told me about Ms. Rachel's son, he was just the man to do it too.

"Whatever, it's not like I'm *trying* to be alone, but these new niggas are straight up clowns. I'm not about to risk my peace just for some dick." She frowned, and even though I knew she wasn't talking about me, I still automatically thought of my situation with Dre's bum ass. He'd been disturbing my peace for as long as I could remember, and in the name of love or not trying to be lonely I'd allowed it. Our relationship had definitely lasted way longer than it needed to, and I'd lost a lot in the process of trying to be his ride or die. From the moment I'd brought him around Dream hadn't liked him though, and that should've told me something. She'd seen us go through some shit and what she didn't see I told her about, so she had good reason to feel the way she did about him. Dream was good at masking those feelings, whenever I'd end up taking him back though. That's just the type of big sister she was, always having my back even when she knew I was doing something stupid. I was just glad that I'd finally gotten rid of dude's dumbass though, and things were looking up, but they'd be looking even better if Dream would hook me up with Ms. Rachel's other son.

"Well, this guy seems nice annnnnd his mama will be something like our new partner so I can't see him being a clown. You must not think so either since you agreed to another date. Hopefully, you'll let him bust that thing open."

"Bitch!" she shrieked and swatted my arm while I laughed. "I'm not fuckin him on the second date!"

"From what you told me, you was damn near about to on the first." I shrugged. "In the words of the late R. Kelly, *I don't see nothing wrooooooong with a little bump and griiiiiind!*" I twerked in my seat and stuck my tongue out playfully.

"He ain't dead fool!"

"You know what I mean." Dream shook her head, and I waved her ass off as she pulled into the parking space in front of the new shop behind a gold Lexus. Flipping down the visor, I checked myself out one last time, before blowing a kiss in the mirror and flipping my 32-inch bundles over my shoulder. Dream had told me that Ms. Rachel was cool as hell and really down to earth, so I knew we would get along great. I was dressed to impress in a pair of butterscotch- colored, high-waisted leather pants, and a cream long sleeve bodysuit, with kitten heels in the same color. I'd taken extra care to make sure that my brows and lashes were on point as well as my light beat. I was sure to make a good impression.

Dream was equally fabulous in a cream sweater dress with butterscotch, knee-length boots. She had her hair in a sleek high bun, and only some nude lipstick to set it all off. We were moving on to a new chapter in our lives, and we were dressing the part.

"Okay now don't be up in here asking this lady about her son. Did you bring your half of the money?" Dream turned to me as we stood waiting for Ms. Rachel to let us in.

"Yes, I have my money, and wasn't nobody even thinkin' about her son." I half lied and shook my purse. I really was going to ask her about her other son, but if Dream thought that it would be unprofessional, then I wouldn't. She gave me a look as if she knew my ass was lying but didn't say anything as the door swung open, and a beautiful older woman greeted us with a smile.

"Hey there Dream." She gushed, pulling my sister in for a hug before turning to me with open arms. "You must be Destiny, I've heard so much about you." Surprised by the affection, I eased into the embrace and was immediately put at ease. Ms. Rachel's hug was warm and genuine, instantly putting me in the mind of a mother figure. Once she released me, she stepped back and allowed us further inside.

"It's so nice to meet you," I told her bashfully, before taking a look around. The pictures that Dream had shown me hadn't done the place justice, and I was completely blown away. Pride covered Ms. Rachel's face, at my reaction.

"I take it you like it?"

"Like it? Ma'am, I'm in love." I couldn't believe that we had lucked out on such a nice salon, and the all we had to do was allow her to come in and work sometimes. It was almost too good to be true.

"Oh, call me Rachel." She giggled with a curt wave. "Come on back to the office, and we can go over the paperwork and things."

I looked at Dream excitedly, with a smile so wide it hurt as we followed her through the salon and into the office she had set up in the back. She'd set the place up nicely and just knowing that it was seconds from being ours had me giddy as fuck.

"This is my lawyer, I'yanna. She'll be here to make sure that you guys are okay with the agreement." Ms. Rachel introduced us to the woman in the room who stood upon us entering. I'yanna was cute. She was caramel-skinned and tall, with a short hair cut that made her look a lot like Eva Pigford, and she was wearing the hell out of a dark blue pantsuit with a silky white blouse underneath. With her nose in the air, she reached across the table to give us both a dainty, handshake, but I could already see that she didn't like us.

"Hi, I'm Dream, and this is my sister Destiny." Dream spoke, breaking the awkward silence that had filled the room after Ms. Rachel's introduction. I wasn't going to fake the funk with her ass though. I could definitely put out the same energy she was, and I planned to. She gave a dry ass "hey" followed up with a phony ass smile, and then returned to her seat. Obviously I'yanna didn't know that while Dream may have been the poised sister, I was the one that got in a bitch's ass, and I'd only allow her to snub us but so many times. I didn't take disrespect well, and if she kept it up, she would learn that with a quickness.

"Well, let's all sit."

Ms. Rachel could tell that the moment was tense and was trying to diffuse things. Dream shot me a warning look, as we both took our seats because she knew I didn't play that shit, but I would behave….for now.

Thirty minutes later, I had managed to keep my attitude in check, despite I'yanna's slick comments. I was actually proud of myself because normally I would have snatched her ass across the desk and beat her out the cheap ass shoes she was rocking, but I kept my cool. That was until it was time to hand over the money. Simultaneously, Dream, and I reached for our wallets, and while she pulled out a fresh cashier's check, I pulled out a knot of cash wrapped with a rubber band.

"Typical." I'yanna scoffed rolling her eyes in my direction.

"Excuse me?" I reared back with my grip tightening around the money I held.

"Nothing." She huffed. "Can you count that out so that I can make sure it's all there at least."

"I know it is, but if you want to make sure then you can count it yourself!" Angrily I tossed the money across the table wishing that I could have hit her in the face with it.

"Destiny!" my sister hissed grabbing ahold of my arm to try and settle me down.

"No, no its alright ladies. I'yanna, I trust these girls, and I'm sure it's all there." Ms. Rachel jumped in instantly making the snide smirk drop from that bitch's face. "Now if that's all, I'll see you girls tomorrow morning." She stood, and we followed suit, with me tossing a nasty look in I'yanna's direction. It felt good to know that Ms. Rachel had our backs and I liked her even more.

She ushered us out of the room, letting I'yanna know that she was walking us out and would be back shortly. Being petty, I stuck my tongue out at her as we left, knowing that we would have problems in the future if we had to be in a room with her again.

"Don't mind I'yanna." Ms. Rachel told us as we made our way to the front. "Sometimes she can be a bit much, but she's like that every time a new woman comes around. She's been trying to be a part of this family since the boys hired her. I don't know what they have going on, but I'll be sure to let Elijah know about her attitude."

"Oh no, it's ok. You don't need to do that." Dream said quickly.

"I absolutely do, and I will. Now you girls go get some rest because tomorrow will be very eventful." She admonished handing over a set of keys to Dream and to me. I clutched mine tightly and squealed gleefully.

"Not so fast, booboo." I'yanna came storming her way towards us, waving around my money. "I'm not sure if this was some type of joke or something, but you're missing about $4,800 from this!" when she stopped she handed me the bills in her hand, and I could clearly see that she was holding two, one hundred dollar bills and the rest was paper cut up to the size of actual money. My mouth fell open shocked as I looked over the contents.

"This ain't what I gave you! Where's my fuckin money, bitch!" I snapped angrily lunging at her, only to be held back by Dream.

"Girl, please! What reason would I have to do something like that? Obviously, you weren't keeping your money in a bank, so you need to go find out who knew where you kept it and check them."

As if a light switch had gone off, Dre instantly came to mind. He was the only one that knew about the money and had access to my house. He'd already tried once to give my money to Juice and Eazy, so what was to stop him from trying to take it himself? It wasn't like he had shit to lose considering that I'd broken up with him and put him out. At first, he didn't seem mad, because he probably thought that we would get back together like we always did, but after seeing Juice at my door that night, he'd had a fit and left angrily. Come to think of it I hadn't heard from him since then. Could it have been because he'd brought his bum ass back to steal my money? With a growl that showed just how pissed I was, I stormed off as Dream apologized on my behalf and promised to get to the bottom of things. I didn't know how I'd allowed myself to get caught slipping. Usually, I counted out my money every day just to make sure that it was all there, but since Dre was no longer in the house, I didn't feel the need to anymore, and that was my fuck up. I could admit that I had slacked a little since he'd moved out, but the fact that he would even do some shit like that, knowing how important that money was to me had me baffled. Furiously, I dialed his number, only to be met with by the voicemail each time. Either he had me blocked, or he was ignoring me, but either way, he would have to see me about my money, and I put that on my son.

* * *

HOURS LATER, when Dream dropped me off after we'd rode around looking for Dre with no luck, I paced my living room fighting back the tears. The fact that he was suddenly unreachable was even more evidence that he was the one that had brought his ass in my house and stolen my money. For the millionth time, I checked his social media accounts, which had been inactive all day and finally got some luck on his Snap. I grit my teeth as I watched him flashing a wad of money with a group of his broke ass friends. It looked like they were in a strip club judging from the slew of naked bitches around them, the loud music, and the strobe lights. I replayed his story at least five times, trying to see if I could gauge which club he was in, only growing more livid as he added videos and pictures with *my* money! I'd long since changed out of my professional clothes and had traded them in for fighting ones. Judging by the sweats I wore you would know that I was ready to fuck somebody up and I was.

Even though me and Dre had, had our spats over the years, both physical and verbal this was sure to be the worst of them all. He knew how much that money meant to me. It was financial freedom. It was hours upon hours away from my son. It was essential! And he'd thrown it away at a damn strip club! I wanted to tell myself that it was unbelievable what he had done, but if I was being honest, this was just like him. A bum ass nigga would try and ruin your dreams, and Dre was the epitome of a bum.

My eyes zeroed in on the table in one of his videos, and I immediately recognized the name Booty Club on a coaster that sat on it. The Booty Club was a new strip joint that he'd begged me on numerous occasions to apply for since my body was stacked and I could dance my ass off. Every time he mentioned it though I refused because while I didn't knock the next woman's hustle, I knew the shit wasn't for me. Plus, I had a whole son out here that could probably see me somewhere shaking my ass. Besides his prodding seemed real pimpish to me and if he thought I was gone get on a pole to make him money he had me fucked up.

After reading the coaster, I was slipping on my Air Maxes as I wrapped my hair up into a ponytail and threw on my jacket to leave. With my keys in hand I stormed to the door only to be met by Yo'Sahn, with an evil looking Juice behind him. He immediately recognized the anger on my face even though Yo'Sahn didn't. He was too busy tryna rush to his room to play some game they'd gotten from the store. I'd been getting more comfortable with the idea of them hanging out, and Juice and his brother didn't seem as bad as that first introduction had made me believe.

"Hey ma, I'm bouta go play this, Juice got me Call of Duty!" Yo'Sahn paused long enough to plant a kiss on my cheek before running to his room. I watched him until he was out of sight in an attempt to avoid Juice's piercing gaze.

"What's wrong?" He questioned reading me despite my avoidance. I really didn't need him further judging me. At this point, I just wouldn't be able to take it. With my head down, I focused on my keys and tried to blink back the tears that were threatening to fall under his scrutiny.

"Nothing, I just didn't know you guys were coming back so soon." I lied hoping that he couldn't pick up on the slight tremble in my voice. Grumbling, he blew out a harsh breath.

"Aye man tell me what the fuck wrong with you before I stop asking nicely!" He demanded. Without looking I could tell his mean ass was frowning and I rolled my eyes at the fact that he thought that was nice. Chuckling bitterly at how bad his attitude was I met his gaze with a heated one of my own.

"I said nothin'! Nobody told yo rude ass to ask in the first place." I was already mad as hell, and I didn't need him adding to it by being an asshole when I was dealing with the shit from Dre. It felt like I had no control over anything that was going on

78

in my life, especially my mixed emotions about him. Juice was good at making me feel like he gave a fuck and then turning around and treating me like one of the bops chasing behind him.

"You know what, you sholl right." He shook his finger at me with a smirk that looked more like a sneer, before turning to leave.

"Okay, wait!" Juice paused at the door but didn't turn around. "Remember that money Dre was trying to give you and your brother the day y'all came? Well, I was saving it for a down payment on a business, and he *stole* it! Now he all in some strip club spending my shit and I'm going to lose out on an opportunity because of his ass!" Again my voice trembled with emotion pissing me off even more. I wasn't a super emotional female. Crying was not something that I did, not even when Dre had hurt me. Anger had always been the way I dealt with shit, but this betrayal was the worst thing he could have ever done. He was fucking with my future, and I had no idea how I'd be able to get back what he'd taken.

"You for real tryna start a business?" Juice asked finally looking at me with a hint of admiration in his eyes as I nodded.

"We met with the lady today to pay and get the keys, but I was short-."

"How much?" he cut me off dismissively and reached into his pocket like he had whatever amount I would need on him.

I squinted in suspicion. "It was five thousand." With a scoff, he pulled out two knots and held them out to me.

"Take it." He ordered once he realized that I wasn't about to accept it. Glancing between him and the money I couldn't help but wonder why he was offering it, and it had me hesitant to accept. Sighing heavily, at my reluctance Juice shoved the money in my hand and left, grumbling that he would be back.

JUICE

*J*left Destiny's crib in search of Dre's bitch ass. I didn't
even know the full details of what he had going on
with her, and I was ready to go fuck him up. If it hadn't been for
him giving us the money he owed us, he would have been dead,
but now it had me wondering if he had taken it from her. That
and the fact that shorty was damn near in tears had me reaching
into my pockets to replace what he'd taken. A part of me felt like
she should have known better than to still be fucking with dude
after the fight that I'd witnessed, but you couldn't tell these
females shit. A call came through on the bluetooth that Yo'Sahn
had hooked up when I'd taken him to Dave and Buster's a few
days before. I'd been trying to keep him busy and out of the
company of Jayden's little ass. It was crazy how Eazy was the
one who originally wanted to look out for him, but I'd ended up
having him with me more. After accepting the call, Eazy's voice
filled the car with a loud ass movie in the back.

"Aye bro, why I'm just now hearing about that shit out west?"

"Nigga cause you wasn't answering yo phone, had me callin'
you like I was one of yo bitches." I sucked my teeth at the
thought. "It's been taken care of tho so that shit don't even

matter." Savion and his homeboy were nothing more than a memory and hopefully a lesson to them other nigga's that I didn't play about my money. I hated that he had even brought the shit up.

"It do matter muhfucka, y'all had it out in broad daylight with a ton of people around!" he grit angrily trying to keep his voice down. I wasn't sure who he was around at the moment, but it was obvious that he didn't want them to hear our conversation.

"Muhfuckas know better than to ever bring my name up in shit-."

"You don't know what somebody will say if the price is right! Don't ever think a nigga or bitch won't sell yo ass out for their own benefit. I told you this, you gotta think before you act bro we not lightweight no more." He was in full lecture mode, but everything he was saying was going in one ear and out the other. I'd been just as deep in the game as him and had never had a problem handling my own.

"You called me to whine about that old shit or did you actually want something, cause I'm already in the middle of some shit." I pulled up to the strip club that was closest to Destiny's crib called Club Supreme and put my car in park.

"Man fuck you, I was actually calling cause you need to talk to that bitch I'yanna. She was on some jealous shit earlier when my girl, and her sister went to pay mama for the shop. I know she only did that goofy shit cause you fucked her, with yo slow ass."

I absentmindedly frowned as I watched some niggas walking to their car with a couple of bitches. None of them were who I was looking for though so I tuned back into the conversation. I'yanna was a lawyer that Eazy had hooked our mama up with back when we first started getting money. From the first day I met her, I could tell she was a thirsty ass hoe, but that ain't stop me from testing her out. She openly flirted with us both, and since Eazy wasn't biting, I decided to. For her to have been so pressed though her pussy wasn't all that and she barely knew how to suck dick. I only fucked with her a handful of times before I finally dropped her ass off my roster and I'd been avoiding her calls ever since. Why Eazy thought that I should be the one to check her in this situation was beyond me. It wasn't like she had a position in my life, she was just a bitch I used to fuck on sometimes, which is exactly what I told him.

"Cause, if you hadn't fucked her then she wouldn't have acted an ass today. Dream already salty cause her sister's bum ass nigga stole her half of the money for their down payment-."

"What! Repeat that shit again." I'd been half listening to him as I texted Grim to tell him and the other niggas in our camp to be on the lookout for Dre, while simultaneously watching the door. A couple of things Eazy said though had me instantly giving him my undivided attention. First of all, he was mentioning his "girl", and he hadn't told me shit about him dating anybody since he'd kicked Sherice's hoe ass to the curb. Secondly, and probably most important was the whole story about her sister's nigga taking some money for a down payment. Destiny's crying ass instantly came to mind, and I shook my head in disbelief. There was no way he was fucking with shorty sister.

"I said if you-."

"Naw, the other part man." I interrupted him irritably. "What girl nigga and what's her sister name?"

"See now you got her lookin' at me all crazy and shit." He laughed before he mumbled some shit in the background and then came back on the line. "She don't think she my woman yet, but her sister name is Destiny."

Damn. So, Destiny had been trying to buy my mama's shop this whole time, and I hadn't even known. I briefly wondered why she hadn't told me, but then again I hadn't really been fucking with her like that since seeing Dre at her house that night after I came to apologize about Makalah's ass.

"How the fuck you ain't know that her sister is Yo'Sahn's mama nigga?" baffled I rubbed a hand down my face.

"Yo'Sahn?" he questioned, and I could hear the frown in his voice followed quickly by a bunch of shuffling in the background and the muffled sounds of old girl talking loudly. That further confirmed for me that I was right about the connection. "Aye let me call you back."

The line beeped indicating that he hung up before I could say shit else, and immediately a text came through from Grim. I nodded, seeing a picture of Dre's bitch ass in the strip club surrounded by bitches. With him located, I sped away from the parking spot and made my way to The Booty Club.

As soon as I got there, Grim was smoking as he waited for me out front. I tucked my gun into my jeans and met him at the door. "How many?"

"It's him and like three other niggas." He informed, blowing out a cloud of smoke.

I stopped looking for cameras long enough to give him the stale face. "Is it three or like three nigga?"

"Might be more," he shrugged lamely. "It's niggas moving in and out the VIP he in so I can't really tell, but you know all them niggas some hoes so…" His voice trailed off, and he went to take another hit off his blunt, but I slapped it out of his hand roughly.

"I don't know shit! You can't underestimate no-fuckin-body!" I grit sounding just like Eazy. What he was saying was true, every nigga that Dre ran with was a bitch just like him, but that didn't mean that one of them wouldn't pull shit. Grim's face showed his discontent at me smacking his blunt out of his hand.

"Mannn, you already know you thinkin' too hard about this shit, but yo ass owe me another blunt Juice for real."

"Yeah, ayite, hype ass probably already got another one

tucked somewhere." I waved his big ass off. Eazy and I were both tall standing at 6'2, but Grim had us beat by at least a foot. That didn't stop me from fucking with him whenever the opportunity presented itself. With him talking shit as he followed behind me, I made my way through the club's door, bypassing security like I owned that bitch. It took no time at all to spot Dre and his flunkies, tossing out bills like he ain't have a care in the world. He'd only owed us a couple of racks so if he stole Destiny's money, he had more than enough left over to be in there flexing. I watched him for a second before making my way over and lifting the velvet rope to let myself in. He didn't notice me right away, but when he did, his eyes bucked in surprise. Playing it off well, he tried to greet me with a hand-shake, but I hit him with a right so swift and hard that he instantly fell backwards onto the couch behind him. All his homies backed away, but I caught one trying to approach me out of the corner of my eye. Before I could pull my gun, Grim knocked him out his shoes. The commotion had a wave of high-pitched screams erupt around the club as naked bitches scurried to get away from the danger.

My brother had just told me to be more careful, but that was the furthest thing in my mind as I beat Dre mercilessly. Out of breath and with a sore fist, I finally stopped hitting him once I saw that he lost consciousness. "Carry this nigga out!"

I barked the order to Grim and swaggered back out of the VIP. The owner of the club quickly walked over with a look of worry on his face.

"I ain't tryna hear shit Ryan, I got you on the damages, and you already know what to do." I gave him a dark look, letting him know that I meant for him to cover that shit up, just as Grim came by carrying Dre out. Ryan nodded his under-standing with his eyes on them. I wasn't worried about him saying shit because he knew that he could very well be in Dre's shoes if he didn't keep his mouth shut.

By the time I made it out, Grim was already in his car, and I knew that he had put Dre in the trunk. I told him to meet me at the warehouse before getting in my car and heading there myself. The whole time my phone blew up with calls from both Destiny and Yo'Sahn's phones. It didn't take a rocket scientist to know that it was her ass trying to be nosy, so I ignored each one. I was still trying to wrap my mind around the fact that I was gone kill this nigga because of her. I tried to reason that I was doing this more so from him paying us with stolen money, but that was bullshit. Destiny had me out here doing shit on her behalf, and she wasn't even my bitch. That didn't stop me from driving my ass out to the warehouse where Grim was waiting and sending a series of shots into his open trunk killing Dre's ass.

"Nigga damn, you couldn't wait till I pulled his ass out!" Grim snapped looking at me in disbelief.

"Nope. Get rid of that shit, the car too. Don't nobody drive caddy's like that no more nigga!" I teased getting in my car, and pulling off while he stood talking shit.

EAZY

"*S*o, let me get this straight. That lil nigga that came up to the Y that day is Juice girl's son, and she's your girl sister, and they tryna buy ma's shop?" Trell asked in disbelief as he sparked up a blunt.

"Hell yeah," I confirmed shaking my head at the shit myself. How I'd been fucking around with Yo'Sahn's Aunty this whole time and didn't know was crazy as fuck to me. Sure, I'd been to her crib, and we'd gone out, but there weren't any signs of Yo'Sahn or her sister there, and whenever she brought up her nephew, she always referred to him as Yoshi. In this day and age, I could understand her wanting to be standoffish as far as letting me too close, it wasn't like I'd been totally open about every aspect of my life either, but at the same time I didn't like it.

Shit seemed to line up almost too perfectly, and I had to wonder why. It could've very well been my paranoia from years in the streets that had me unsure of things, but I would always rather be safe than sorry. Besides the way she turned up at the mention of Yo'Sahn's name the other night had me looking at her different. If I didn't know any better, I would assume that she knew about my street ties. The fact that Dre's girl knew exactly what I was into was reason enough for me to speed up telling her myself cause I knew she wouldn't hesitate to. I'd planned to ease it on her after she'd fallen for me or possibly not say shit at all, but there was no way I could go about it that way now.

"Damn, shit crazy." Trell mused handing the blunt over to me. I didn't say shit as I accepted it because he said exactly what I was thinking. As if I'd thought her up a text came through from Dream and despite being in midday traffic, I rushed to see what it said. I hadn't talked to her since the other night when Juice dropped that bomb on me. I'd gone over there to try and smooth shit over after the fiasco at the shop and let her know that my mama wasn't tripping since she'd been ignoring her calls. Really, I just wanted to lay eyes on her fine ass, but almost immediately she started going off about what had happened. That's how I'd ended up staying and calming her down to the point that she agreed to chill and watch a movie with me. It was an impromptu date, but I was taking anything I could get at this point.

Mine: I just wanted to let you know that my sister got the money, she won't say how but I already talked to Ms. Rachel and let her know too!

Me: that's what's up. So, does that mean I can still see you this weekend?

I watched as the bubbles popped up like she was about to say something before disappearing making my eyebrows bunch together.

"Man watch the fuckin road nigga!" Trell shouted, and I looked up just in time to stop, barely missing the minivan in front of us. "Fuck is you doin! You ain't sposed to be textin' and drivin' no way!" He fussed snatching the blunt from my lips.

"Shut yo scary ass up, I stopped, didn't I?"

"Barely! You and Juice don't need no damn girlfriends, they knockin' both y'all off y'all square!" Hands shaking he took a couple deep pulls off the blunt. "I hope Budda can talk some sense into yo ass for real." He grumbled referring to my mentor that we were on our way to see. I hadn't been up to the prison to visit him in a few months due to business being hectic, but today was his birthday, so I made sure to have time. Budda was five years older than me and had taken me under his wing back when I first decided to jump in the drug game. He taught me the ropes and always had a gem to drop. While I had my father, it had been easier to talk to Budda about shit that I was going through. He gave me advice about girls, niggas at school, my future. At first, he tried to discourage me from following in his footsteps, but it was like talking to a brick wall. Eventually, he figured out that I wasn't trying to hear none of that shit and instead of having me try and do things on my own, and possibly end up dead, he taught me everything I needed to know.

He got jammed up a couple of years ago when he got pulled over with a gun in the car. Since he had such a good lawyer on retainer, and the gun was clean, he got off with much less time than he could have gotten.

Since then, me and Juice's empire had grown even bigger. I knew he was proud of how far I'd come, but at the same time, we'd need to figure out a role for him once he touched back down. One thing I knew for sure was that the law was gone be on his ass, and I didn't want that type of heat around my shit. He'd already been talking about his release and jumping head first back into things. I was still thinking of an easy way to let him know that it wasn't going to happen in my camp. I would do what I could and make sure he was straight, but as far as the streets went it was a no go.

That shit had been the furthest thing from my mind, especially since I had Dream renting up so much space there, but the closer we got to the jail, the more it came to the forefront. Sighing, I stuffed my phone down into my pocket and resigned myself to worrying about her later.

"Dream ain't doin' shit nigga, I'm on top of everything."

"Aw yeah? Then how you ain't know about Juice and what happened out West. I'm pretty sure he did that shit cause his shorty's son was over there getting his lil ass beat." He looked at me pointedly.

"That's-."

"What about him killin' that nigga Dre at the strip club?" Trell asked cutting me off. I looked back and forth between him and the street trying to see if he was just fucking with me. It had to be some type of joke because I'd just had a conversation with Juice about this shit. The look on Trell's face told me that he was serious and my hard-headed ass little brother had gone and killed this nigga at a strip club!

"I'm gone fuck that nigga up!" I gritted angrily and punched the steering wheel. Here I was ready to tell Budda that his presence would bring more attention to us when he got out and Juice was out here making shit hot all on his own. I had a mind to skip this damn visit and go straight over to fuck that nigga up, but I'd already made it this far. Trell laughed at my outburst and shook his head.

"Yo calm your angry ass down fuck you beating on the car like that for! This a Wraith nigga, not no damn Honda!" he was petting the dashboard like it was a pet and not a car, and I wanted to slap his ass too. None of Juice's antics ever bothered him, in fact, most of the time he thought the shit was funny, now was exactly one of those times.

"Ain't shit funny! He out here reckless as hell and I been told him to tone that shit down." I grumbled as I pulled into the parking lot of the prison, suddenly in an even worse mood. I couldn't wait to talk to his ass.

Trell shrugged and put the blunt out. "I mean, that's just who that nigga is. You had to know he wasn't gone listen to shit you had to say."

I guess I could understand why he would say that, but it didn't stop me from mugging him hard as hell. Even if Juice didn't want to listen to me, he still should've had better self-preservation than to be out here murking people in broad daylight. Without saying anything, I got out and made my way inside with Trell following closely behind. I wasn't trying to get into a full-blown debate about my kid brother, at least not right now I wasn't.

After a special visit to the warden to drop off Budda's birthday present, we sped through the process of being searched before finally entering the visitation room. Budda was already sitting at one of the round tables, but once he saw us he stood with a wide grin.

"Look at y'all niggas, walking in here like big money!" He guffawed giving each of us a one armed hug.

"You know how I do." Trell soaked up the compliment while I just smiled modestly. I was never the type to brag about money and shit. One of the main things that Budda had taught me was to keep a low profile, and for the most part, I did. His comment about big money was him acknowledging the fact that I was dressed modestly. Budda's lessons had been instilled in me, and my plain black Henley and light wash Levi's with black timbs showed him that.

"Happy birthday man," I told him. "I already dropped your gift off, don't forget to get it."

"Yeah happy birthday, big homie. You getting old ain't ya!" Trell added.

"Ain't shit on me old nigga! I could take your bitch!" Budda said making us all laugh.

"Shiiiit, the way these hoes be going you probably could!" Trell backed down easily.

"Damnnn right." Budda nodded motioning for us to sit

down. "Where Juice's wild ass at?" He asked once we'd all taken a seat.

"Mannnn you know that nigga be in the wind," I replied, running a hand down my waves, and looking around the room. It was full of visitors, women and kids all dressed up to see the man in their lives and the occasional mother there to see her son. That was one of the most fucked up parts about coming there for me, seeing all the broken families having to see their loved ones locked down.

"Yeah, lil nigga always been hard to keep up with. When I touch down, I'm gone have to get him together like how I did you." He said with a chuckle, but I knew he was only half joking. The problem was that despite what he thought Juice would be much harder to "get together" than I was. Juice and Budda used to get along great until Budda got jammed and then it slowly began to go downhill. After a few years, he wasn't tryna answer Budda's calls or come see him. I always figured it was because it was just something he didn't feel like keeping up with, but knowing Juice there was no telling.

"These niggas out here getting cuffed, shit got them all fucked up too. I barely recognize their ass." Trell snickered. I shot an evil glare his way, but he was completely unfazed as he continued to talk shit.

"Shantell finally got you to act right, huh?" Budda asked with a wide grin as I shook my head adamantly.

"Hell naw that hoe been canceled! Crazy ass bitch." I mumbled that last part not bothering to correct him on Sherice's name.

"Aw yeah?" He seemed surprised as his eyebrows damn near met his hairline. "Who's the lucky lady then? I know she gotta be bad as hell to knock Shantell out her spot." He pressed.

"Nigga you mean Sherice?" Trell jumped in, and Budda shrugged indifferently.

"It ain't no lucky nothin'. Trell putting more on that shit than necessary, ain't nobody out here cuffin' shit, I'm just living." The lie rolled off my tongue before I could stop it, and I really don't know where it came from. The truth was I was definitely trying to make things official with Dream and as soon as I left there, I was going straight to her crib. Why I was avoiding telling Budda about her, I didn't know, but it just seemed like I should keep it to myself for now.

"Don't be so against a relationship Eazy, my shorty the best thing that ever happened to me. I can't wait to get out and start a family and shit." He boasted proudly. I'd never met Budda's woman, Shay, but I remember him always bragging on her to anybody that would listen. Word was he kept her locked away from the street shit so nobody could ever hurt her on his account, not even me. The closest I'd come to seeing her was the night he got arrested he'd just dropped off some work to me, and she was in the car, but I couldn't see her behind the heavy tint. I guess we thought the same way because I wanted to keep Dream all to myself too.

"Mannn this nigga tryna turn us into some uncles and shit!" Trell teased with a laugh.

"You ain't gone be no uncle to my shorties! Probably have my kids out here cussin' and throwing up gang signs and shit!"

"I wouldn't do no shit like that!" Trell feigned hurt. "I might use em to get some hoes, but all that other shit, nah. That's what Juice would be on!"

"Aw hell naw! I'm keeping both y'all niggas away from my kids!" Budda laughed. "But on some real shit a nigga gone be touching down soon so tell the streets to be ready." He smirked sneakily. I was ready to question him more about his release date because as far as I knew he had another year and a half left, but the guards yelled out that the visit was over and I reluctantly had to let it go. As we stood and said our goodbyes, I made a note to call his lawyer and find out if he would be getting out earlier. I'd missed the opportunity to talk to him about his position upon release, but if he was being released sooner, then I'd have to get on that ASAP.

DREAM

"So, you really not gone tell me how you got the money?" I asked Destiny for the hundredth time since we'd been on the phone. I knew good and damn well that Dre's bum ass hadn't given it back. It seemed weird for her to just come up on that type of cash out of nowhere, and my nosey nature just wouldn't let me leave it alone. Another call came through from Elijah, and I quickly ignored it. He'd been calling me since I texted him earlier, but I wasn't ready to deal with him just yet. I didn't know what to think about him knowing Yo'Sahn. It gave me stalker vibes, and I already dealt with a controlling ass nigga before. Him knowing things about me that I hadn't divulged was suspect and one of the signs that I'd missed in my previous relationship. So, until I got to the bottom of it, I wasn't going to be on a personal level with him, but something told me with a man like Elijah that would be easier said than done.

"Bitch I didn't do nothing illegal so why does it matter." She quipped snapping me back into the conversation, with a suck of her teeth, and I could tell she was rolling both her eyes and neck.

Sighing I decided to drop it….. for now. The important thing was that we'd gotten our location and were set to open soon. "Okay, okay. You're right as long as it's nothing that's gone have us locked up then I'll leave it be. Now, where's nephew?" I asked grinning widely.

"He's uh…he's at Jalen's." She stuttered making my eyes narrow suspiciously. Destiny was acting funny as hell, and I wondered if she was talking back to Yoshi's daddy or something. That would definitely explain how she'd gotten the money, and where my nephew had been disappearing to lately. I'd been meaning to hang out with him sometime recently because I hadn't seen him in a while, but it seemed like shit just kept coming up.

"Oh, wellll I got him the new Call Of Duty so-."

"Aw, he already got it Juuuuu-. I-I bought it for him the other day." Her voice became high pitched as she tried to cover up what she was about to say.

"Aht aht bitch! Who you was bouta say?" I questioned quickly just as loud knocking sounded at my door. Frowning, I looked in its direction and tried to will whoever it was away. I wasn't expecting company, and I wasn't in the mood to entertain either. There were still fliers that I needed to make and ads that I needed to post online so that I could get employees and clients. Rachel had said that she only had four stylists working and hadn't promised them a position once she retired so it would be totally up to Destiny and me if we decided to keep them. Me being the type that knew how important your coins were was willing to give them a trial run, but we still needed to fill up the other two chairs plus find another lash and brow tech.

"Go answer your door, I'll call you back later!"

"You bet not hang up this phone-!"

Beep! Beep! Beep!

I was met by the three beeps that let me know she'd done

just that. I pulled the phone away from my ear and grumbled obscenities as I stomped childishly to the door and swung it open without looking through the peephole. "Who-!"

My words got stuck in my throat at the sight of Elijah King standing on my doorstep with anger evident on his face. Without giving me a chance to gather myself, he stepped inside, invading my space, and dizzying me with the smell of his cologne.

"Why you been ignoring my calls." He asked piercing me with those chocolate orbs as he kicked the door shut behind him. Despite the look on his face, his voice was low and calm like he was trying to control his anger. With me backed against the wall, he planted his hands on each side of my head, so I could no longer avoid his gaze. As much as I hated to admit it, my body reacted to him immediately. He wasn't even touching me, but already my nipples were straining against the thin fabric of my t-shirt. I could try and blame it on the cold air that came in with him, but the truth was, Elijah just oozed sex and an underlying thug appeal that had me full of lustful thoughts whenever he was around. The things I was feeling for him after such a short period of time scared me, and that was the reason why I was ignoring him, and making excuses as to why I couldn't or shouldn't trust him. The last time I'd felt anything close to this was with my ex, and that nigga was the worst mistake of my life! I wasn't trying to go down that road again.

"I haven't-."

"So we lying now?" He asked cutting me off with an amused chuckle.

"I mean, it's not like you've been telling the whole truth." I shot back.

"This about Yo'Sahn? I told you I was starting a mentorship thing the first time I took you out. He's the kid I was talking about. What? Was I supposed to ask you if you knew him or some shit?" His voice raised slightly as he cocked his head with a confused frown.

"It's not just that." I huffed, trying to buy myself time. I couldn't think clearly with him so close to me. Slipping out from under his arm, I put some distance between us by damn near running into the living room. I'm sure I looked crazy as hell to him, but I wasn't ready to fall yet, and Elijah King was making it so damn hard not to.

"What else is it Dream, and don't come with no bullshit either! Let's figure this out now, so we can move past it and get back to our vibe." He said and removed his coat and hat before making himself comfortable on my sofa. As he sat back and adjusted himself, I zeroed in on the print in his gray, Nike sweats and licked my lips lustfully. The move didn't go unnoticed by Elijah. He smirked up at me confidently and leaned forward, planting both elbows on his knees, and blocking my view in the process.

"Is that what this all about? You need some dick huh?" His grin grew wider.

"What! No-."

"Oh really? I bet you soaking wet right now." He mused, grabbing ahold of my hand and pulling me into his lap. I couldn't lie, my lace thongs were definitely ruined and no doubt my desire had seeped through the thin biker shorts I wore. Immediately I could feel his dick growing beneath me, and I tried to get my ass up, but he only held me in place, shifting slightly so that my legs could rest comfortably on each side of him.

"Elijah I-." My words were stolen by a deep kiss that had me moaning into his mouth as his tongue danced with mine. Instinctively I wrapped my arms around his neck getting more into it while his warm hands slid under my shirt, cupping my breasts and squeezing, sending a shudder down my spine. A second later my shirt was off, and the friction I was creating as I ground against him on the verge of releasing a much needed and well overdue orgasm had me clutching him tightly.

"Ahhhhh!" I whimpered softly and buried my face into Elijah's neck as a wave of euphoria swept over me.

"Now that you got one out the way." He said after I'd finally recovered with my face still hidden, except now it was from shame. I'd brought myself to climax more times than I could count over the last few years, but it was just that. Me doing it for myself. Being so close to a man, one as tempting as Elijah was something else entirely, and I was ashamed of how quickly I'd lost control. Unfazed by my silence, he found my lips again, despite the small fight I put up. This time the kiss was much slower and more passionate, but it didn't lack any of the previous' intensity. With ease, he stood to his feet and carried me further into my apartment checking each door until he found my bedroom. My heart pounded as he laid me down gently, finally breaking our kiss long enough to lick and suck his way down my body. My skin tingled in every spot that he touched and as he reached to pull my shorts down, I raised my hips slightly allowing him to slip them off with ease. Everything came so easy for him it was no wonder that the second his tongue found my throbbing center I was shaking and on the verge of another climax. He stopped just when I was about to reach my peak looking up at me cockily as my juices glistened from his beard.

"Don't." I couldn't stop myself from begging.

"Don't worry beautiful, I ain't nowhere near done." He teased backing away long enough to strip off his clothes and display his chiseled body. The cover of his joggers hadn't done him any justice because his dick was much bigger than I thought. I swallowed the lump in my throat as he tore open a condom that seemed to appear out of nowhere and rolled it on. Even though I was scared of what he could do to me with that monster, I still opened up, clasping my legs around his smooth back as soon as he climbed back on top of me. "Relax, I'm gone take it easy on you," Elijah assured, placing himself at my opening. I nodded despite being anything but relaxed and found his lips again massaging my tongue with his as he maneuvered his way inside of me.

"Mmmm, uhhh!"

I was virgin tight from lack of penetration, but Elijah's girth made it that much more painful even with him going slowly. He removed his mouth from mine, sucking and nibbling on my neck in an effort to distract me, which worked perfectly because the next thing I knew he'd filled me up. The pain mixed with pleasure as he stroked me slow and steady, my pussy fitting him like a glove.

"Shit, Dream." He grunted pushing into me so deep I felt him in my stomach. His husky voice, coupled with his powerful thrusts had me so wet my moans were competing with the sounds of Elijah stirring my middle.

"Ooohmyfuuuuckiinga!" I couldn't even recognize the incoherent babbling I was doing, but I'd *never* experienced sex like this. Seconds later I was exploding yet again, and totally spent, but Elijah wasn't done with me yet. He pulled my limp body up with his so that he was now sitting with me on top, putting pressure right on my g-spot.

"Wake that ass up, and ride this muhfucka!" He growled smacking me on the ass aggressively and nipping into my neck. Still not fully recovered, it took me a minute to get it together and start moving my hips. Once I did though my body came alive, with my feet planted on the bed, I bounced on his dick first slowly and then fast. I threw my head back and arched my back, giving Elijah better access to my nipples. "Damn you so fuckin wet." He moaned sexily.

"Ooooh! I-I'm bouta cummm!" I gasped squeezing my eyes shut as my body quivered uncontrollably.

"Let me feel it then, I'm right behind you," Elijah ordered, his voice muffled within my chest as he drilled into me from underneath. I felt him stiffen even more driving me right over the edge. Still trembling I rested against him, and soon he was squeezing my ass while he came, dick throbbing inside me as he coated the condom with his seeds.

The room was silent besides our heavy breathing. Elijah lifted me slowly off of him, and I winced as he slipped out of me. He laid me back on my pillows with that same cocky ass smirk from before and planted a quick kiss on my lips.

"Told you." He winked before lifting off the bed and disappearing out of my room. I admired his frame as my eyes drooped closed. He had me sleepy as fuck and strung out off one taste of the dick, but at that moment I didn't even care. The bed dipped alerting me of Elijah's return, but I kept my eyes closed figuring that he'd gone to dispose of the condom.

"Nooooo Elijah, let me sleep some first," I whined as he gently opened my legs. Chuckling quietly he kissed the inside of my thigh, causing my clit to throb despite the soreness I felt.

"Can't even hang." His voice held a teasing tone to it, and I can't lie I was anticipating his mouth on me, but instead, I was met with the warmth of a soapy towel. Elijah took his time wiping me clean, and that in itself was sensual as fuck. Once he was done he gently kissed my pussy, and I realized I was ready for round two, or would it be three at this point. I didn't even know, but I was damn sure craving him back between my legs and Elijah came ready to oblige.

THE NEXT MORNING I woke up to Elijah feasting on me as if he hadn't eaten all my pussy up the night before. I was honestly surprised that I even had feeling below my waist at this point.

"Mmmm." I moaned lowly meeting his eyes as he suckled at my clit. It didn't take long for me to drown him in my juices, and we were right back at it. How had I been ready to deprive myself of this I didn't know, but now I was sprung.

As sprung as I was though, the sound of my alarm blaring brought me right out of my sex-induced trance. Today we were meeting with Ms. Rachel and the stylists so that we could get to know each other and work on a plan for the rebranding. I broke away from Elijah's grip and shut off the screeching box on my nightstand, ignoring his groan of protest.

"Damn you tryna run, and I ain't even did shit yet." He looked up at me with a lazy grin, and I fought the urge to climb right back into bed with him.

"Cute but ain't nobody gotta run from you." I sassed rolling my eyes. "I actually need to meet your mother at the shop." I'd been humbled by the dick, but I wasn't about to let it fuck up my money.

"Oh, word? That's what's up gone do your boss shit beautiful." He stroked his full beard and eyed me with admiration, probably not even realizing how sexy his confidence was on him. My ex would have never been so encouraging about me working. He'd always wanted to keep me under his thumb, and the easiest way to do that was by controlling the money. In his mind, if I depended on him solely, then I would never be able to leave. I swear the best thing that ever happened to me was him getting jammed up that day. Brian A.K.A. Budda was controlling and very abusive, that's why it was so easy for me to spot the same characteristics in Dre. When it came to ambition, the two were as different as night and day, but they'd obviously studied from the same manual when it came to the mind games they played. It was a breath of fresh air to be in the presence of a man who wanted me to succeed and saw me as his equal, Elijah was getting brownie points and didn't even know it.

An hour later after a shower that involved a quickie, I stood at my mirror applying a light coat of makeup. I decided to keep it simple since I was already running short on time messing around with Elijah. I wore olive green coveralls with a black, long sleeve tight-fitting shirt underneath and some black, suede booties. After I applied some Revlon super lustrous gloss to my lips, I was ready. My hair hung bone straight with a deep part, with little effort. I was looking good.

"Damn, I don't know if I wanna let yo fine ass leave." Elijah came up behind me, wrapping his arms around my middle and nuzzling my neck. I allowed myself a second to relish in how good he felt before shaking him off.

"Nope, I'm already gonna be late cause you wanted to shower with me. You not about to have Ms. Rachel on my ass." I told him with a roll of my eyes, and he held up his hands in mock surrender. Ten minutes later we were both heading out, with promises to see each other later. I watched him swagger to his car in awe, he looked damn good in the morning's light, even rocking yesterday's clothes. With a grin plastered on my face, I finally climbed into my car and drove off.

DESTINY

$\mathcal{I}$ watched my sister walk over to me with a wide smile. There was no mistaking the limp in her walk and the glow on her face. That bitch had finally gave it up. For a second, I thought I was gone have to hear her mouth about hanging up on her last night and about my half of the money magically appearing, but the second she stepped out of her car I knew I was in the clear.

"Sooooo Ms. Rachel's son sent you off to work the right way, huh?" I teased as soon as she was within earshot. "I'm gone need details bitch!"

"I'm not even gone dignify that with an answer." She said stopping next to me with a roll of her eyes, but I wasn't letting her off the hook that easy.

"But you not denying it though, so you might as well spill the tea cause you know I ain't lettin' up."

"You so damn thirsty." She shook her head as she pulled the keys from her pocket so that she could let us in.

"Sure am." I shrugged unbothered by her insult. The truth of the matter was besides the occasional lustful stare I caught Juice giving me my life had been pretty dry, and my sex life was even worse. If there wasn't shit else that Dre got right, it was the way he pleased my body. Since I hadn't gotten any since we'd broken up I was good and sexually frustrated, so the next best thing was being all up in Dream's business.

"Ugh, fine." She huffed opening the glass door. We made our way inside cutting on the lights, and I followed her over to the first station where she set her things down. I plopped down into the chair right next to her and removed my coat, getting comfortable.

"Okay come on, before everybody else gets here." I gushed once she finally eased into her chair.

"Okay well, it was Elijah at the door last night, and at first he was pissed about me not answering his calls. He got right in my ass about that shit too! Read the fuck out of me and said that I needed some dick-."

"Uh cause you did." I interrupted her with a laugh. She gave me a pointed look, silencing me so that she could finish. I listened as she told me how he'd fucked her into a coma and still had more for her this morning. From the sound of it, Elijah had given her that hood book love and she still had stars in her eyes. "Damnnnn bitch." I sighed once she'd finished.

"I know that shit was almost too good. He gone have me out here strung out."

"I ain't mad at him, yo ass *need* some consistent dick in yo life." I pointed out with a smirk. As far as I knew Dream had been on a drought since Brian's weak ass had gotten locked up, and since that had been years ago, I knew that sis was in serious need of some male attention.

"Mmhmm, but you ain't off the hook though bitch. You still not gone tell me how you got the money? Don't think I forgot." She quipped eyeing me from head to toe. I opened my mouth to speak, unsure of how to answer but thank god the sound of the bell on the door went off alerting us of someone entering the shop. I wasn't ready to let her know about Juice, and I damn sure didn't want to tell her that he was the one that gave me the money. She'd be all up in my business, and although Juice and his brother had taken a liking to Yo'Sahn, they were still thugs who could kill our ass at the end of the day. Dream glared my way but dropped the conversation as Ms. Rachel, and a few other women stepped inside.

"Hi girls, I'm glad to see you're here already you both look very nice." She complimented, giving us each a quick hug.

"Thanks, and you're looking gorgeous as always," I said eyeing the black Banana Republic two-piece pants suit she wore, with a white fur lined cashmere coat. Despite her compliment, I still felt underdressed standing next to her in my dark gray, short sleeve tunic top and black leggings with high top all-white Vans.

"Thanks, sweetie." She cheesed and absentmindedly patted her low bun before turning to the other women in the room. "I'd like you to meet Ashley, Sariah, Gabby and Danielle. You've both already been introduced to I'yanna."

Everyone stepped forward to greet us, I'yanna being the last to come over with a fake ass smile on her face. I wasn't sure what she needed to be present for, but she was the last person I wanted to see. The only good thing about her being there was the fact that I could rub it in her face that I *did* have the money after all.

"Sorry about that little misunderstanding we had last time. Jeremiah and I had a loooong conversation about it, and he ummm set me straight." She smirked, making sure that I caught the double meaning in her words. Why she felt the need to tell me that I wasn't sure, because I hadn't even met Jeremiah, but I was going to assume that he was Rachel's other son. If he fucked with bitches like this though I didn't want to meet him.

Rolling my eyes, I waved her off. "Girl if you don't get the fuck-."

"I'yanna," Ms. Rachel stressed with a stern look.

"Oh, I got this." Dream cut in stepping in front of her. "Uhh I'yanna, I'm sure you're here for a reason, so I'm gonna ask you to do what you came for and not bother my sister with bullshit she ain't worried about." She wiped the smug look right off that bitch's face, and I couldn't have been prouder. Ms. Rachel quickly pulled her to the side and had words with her while Dream shook off the interaction and addressed the stylists. That was something I would need to master, being able to check hoes without immediately wanting to fight and act a fool. Dream had it down to a science, but she'd always been the more chill of us two. I only half listened to her little speech as I tried to simmer down because I didn't want to act out on the first day. Once I saw that I'yanna was heading to the door though my mood shifted and I was able to tune in to what was being said.

As she spoke about booth rent, uniforms, hours, and clients, I eyed the remaining women in the room none of whom seemed at all put off by the scene with I'yanna which let me know that they were used to her being out of pocket. They could be as cool with that hoe's bullshit as they wanted to be, but I wasn't going to tolerate it.

"Hey Destiny, did you want to say something before we get to work?" Dream asked snapping me out of my thoughts. I quickly shook my head no, because her ass put me on the spot, and I wasn't prepared to speak. The look on her face let me know that she was hoping I would, but she played it off well. "Okaaaay. Well ladies I know that you all are ready to get back to work so I won't keep you however we will be changing the sign this next coming week so I'll keep you posted on what day that will be and you can schedule your bookings around the construction otherwise it's been nice meeting you all. Unless you have any questions, then you can get to work."

"Uhhh I got a question." The girl Gabby raised her hand with a hint of attitude. "When is the new uniform taking effect, because I'm gone need time to get some black clothes that I can wear here. I don't even see why our old smocks won't work anyway."

A chorus of groans erupted from the other ladies, but Ashley was the only one to actually speak. "Gabby cut it, you got more than enough money to buy some black clothes." She said sucking her teeth. They all seemed annoyed by her question, and it was clear that she was going to get on my nerves too. I rolled my eyes and resisted the urge to call her ass stupid. I'd seen the old smocks with the previous name on them so it was obvious why they wouldn't work. She was just doing the most.

"I'm just saying. She asked if we had any questions and I think that's a solid one." Gabby shrugged. "Wasn't nobody even talking to you no way Ashley."

"Girl, stop tryna show out, this not what you want." Ashley grit.

"Okay, so y'all both need to calm that all the way down." I found myself saying. "Ain't nobody bouta be fighting. Now Gabby, I'm sure it won't be hard for you to find some black pants and shirts. As far as the smocks go, they'll be different because they will have the new name on them, *our.*" I moved my finger between me and Dream. "Company name. Either you gone adjust to that or you can find another salon to work at."

She grumbled a dry ass okay, and I took that to mean that she was staying. Dream came up beside me with a look of approval, probably relieved that I hadn't resorted to violence to get my point across. I was low key proud of myself too. It had been easier than I'd thought to handle the situation, I just hoped that all the conflicts would be that simple, but with a room full of women I knew that was just wishful thinking.

Ms. Rachel didn't have an appointment that day, so she ended up leaving us to it, and the rest of the day we spent working on fliers and other marketing ideas. After a few hours with them, I realized that Ashley, Danielle, and Sariah were all cool as hell and easy to work with, and Gabby wasn't that bad either once she'd been put in her place. When it was all said and done, we'd gotten a lot accomplished and the time had flown by.

"Hey, I think we deserve some drinks. First round on me." Dream busted out and said after we'd put everything away. Everybody got hyped as hell, and I raised my brows at her surprised. That dick definitely had her in a good ass mood. She'd been giggly and shit the whole day, and I'd even caught her smiling at her phone a few times.

"Ohhhh you in a good, good mood huh?" I teased as we all gathered our things to head out.

"Bitch stop, I'm always in a good mood." She shrugged into her coat, but couldn't hide the silly grin on her face for shit. "Will Yo'Sahn be cool for a little bit while we're out?"

"Yeah, I talked to him after he got home from school, but I'll check with him again on the way," I told her knowing full well that today he was with Juice and his brother playing basketball. They spent so much time with him that I almost never saw my own son, but I also knew that he needed male figures in his life since his daddy wasn't around how he should be. I waited while Dream locked up and then hurried to my car with plans to meet her and the others at the bar down the street.

With the heat on blast, I pulled out my phone to see that I had a missed call from Juice's fine ass. Since my baby was with him, I immediately dialed his number and primped while I waited on him to answer.

"Why you ain't answer when I called?" his deep voice came through sending a shiver down my spine. I always felt like a hot in the ass teenager fucking around with him because everything he said got a reaction out of me. I started to speak, but he cut me off before I could get a word out. "It could've been an emergency with Yo'Sahn or some shit."

Instantly my little bubble burst, and I released an irritated sigh. "Well I was at work, today we met with the other stylists and started working on promotional stuff, so I lost track of time. I called as soon as I got a moment, though." I rolled my eyes as I snapped my visor shut and hooked my phone up to my aux so that I could pull off. Every time I thought that he was showing some type of interest in me, he shut me right down. For whatever reason, it seemed like Juice didn't see me as shit but Yo'Sahn's mama. I really shouldn't have been so pressed for his attention, considering how we met and the type of women he kept company with, but he just did something to me. Ever since he'd come around, things had been looking up. Dre was gone, I had someone spending quality time with my son, and I'd been able to quit both my jobs. He was like a good luck charm, so it was easy for me to get attached, but maybe I needed to stop reading so much into his presence.

"Today *was* your first day, huh? How was it?" he asked, making butterflies swarm my belly once again at the fact that he even cared to ask.

"It was *interesting.* Definitely different from what I'm used to." I admitted with a sigh. Today had opened my eyes to some of the things that I would have to deal with as part owner of a business. My sister made that shit look so damn easy, but it would take time for me to get used to a leadership role after years of working for someone else.

"Why you sound like you doubting yourself shorty?" I could hear shuffling on his end, and after a second the background noise faded, letting me know that he had moved to somewhere quieter.

"I don't know, shit." I shrugged even though I knew exactly why.

"That's what I'm sayin. Just cause it's some new shit don't mean you ain't gone be able to come out on top, just like you been doing. You been out here on your boss shit, takin' care of Yo'Sahn and working two jobs and shit. Don't even get me started on how you was out here being a mother to that grown ass bum." He finished instantly wiping the small smile off my face. It was just like him to give me a compliment and in the same breath talk his shit.

"See why you even have to just do all that." I sucked my teeth as I pulled into the parking spot a few cars down from Dream. It had taken me longer to get there than the rest of them because I was trying to prolong the conversation, but Juice's ignorant ass had to ruin it with his smart mouth.

"Shit, it's true!" he chuckled. "But I made my point though, you got this."

"Awww, let me find out you can be nice when you wanna be." My face hurt from smiling so hard. Juice's evil ass never had nothing nice to say, so hearing him compliment me like that had my heart pounding.

"Ahhhh see now yo ass doing too much bruh. Shouldn't you be off by now, I'm bouta bring my lil homie home." He fussed faking an attitude.

"Actually, I'm bouta grab a drink with my sister and the other girls, but I won't be long. Maybe just an hour or so-."

"A drink? Aye, take yo ass home Destiny! Me and my brother ain't been kickin' it with Yo'Sahn so you can be out here in nigga's faces!" My brows snapped together confused by his change of mood. I didn't know what the fuck his problem was, but he was tripping for no reason.

"Excuse you, ain't nobody even said shit about a nigga! What the fuck is yo problem!"

"Naw excuse you! Ain't shit wrong with me, but you definitely gone have a problem if you don't go the fuck home, and you better beat me there!" he snapped before the phone beeped letting me know he'd hung up. I sat there trying to figure out what the fuck had just happened. We'd been doing so good, and then he just started going off about me being in a nigga's face. That was the shit I was talking about, he kept paying me dust, but then acting like he gave a fuck at the same time. There was just no winning with that crazy ass nigga, but he wasn't about to ruin my night. I was still gone have my drink, and then I'd go home.

"Come on, bitch!" Dream hollered knocking on my window and prompting me to cut my car off and get out. "What took you so long, it's cold as hell out here."

"I told you I was gone call Yoshi." I was still shaken up and irritated by Juice, but I wasn't about to tell her that. She accepted my answer anyway though, only nodding as we made our way inside where Ashley, Sariah, Gabby, and Danielle stood waiting for us in the long hallway.

As soon as we sat down at the table these hoes all started to order girly ass fruity drinks, but I needed mine to count which is why I ordered a double shot of patron and Cîroc with a splash of cranberry.

"Damn you tryna get fucked up ain't you?" Danielle questioned playfully once the waitress left to go fill our orders.

"Nah, she handles her liquor better than anybody I know." Dream grinned knowing how I was. The little bit of shit I'd ordered wouldn't do nothing but put my ass to sleep later. I'd definitely got my tolerance from our mama.

"Facts," I added, catching sight of Sariah and Gabby sharing a look. I started to ask them what the fuck that was all about but decided against it. Juice was enough of a problem already I didn't need another one, not tonight anyway. Thankfully, our drinks came out distracting me, and I wasted no time taking down the shots.

"Oh, I been meaning to ask when the fuck was you gone tell me about this." Dream who'd been all in her phone lifted it so that only I could see a picture of Yo'Sahn with Eazy and Juice. The sip of Cîroc I'd taken went down the wrong pipe at the sight, and I immediately started choking. "Yeah bitch, apparently my boo and his brother have been mentoring him, and you ain't think to tell me. That's why yo ass been being all secretive, and I thought it was cause you had been messing around with Antonio again." She rolled her eyes and nonchalantly took a sip of her Long Island iced tea, while I was still trying to recover from the initial shock. Not only was the man I knew as Eazy, Ms. Rachel's son that my sister had been messing with, but that meant Juice was her other son. Here I was trying to meet the nigga, and I was already well acquainted with him. I wondered if he had known the whole time too and had just been fucking with me. The part that was really bothering me though was that he'd been the one messing with I'yanna. I didn't even see how that had happened, but then again, I didn't see how he was fucking Makaylah either.

"Small world ain't it?" Dream smirked as my phone buzzed in my pocket. I knew it had to be Juice's dumb ass, but I checked anyway just in case it was Yo'Sahn. Seeing me and Yo'Sahn's picture pop up on my screen had me breathing a sigh of relief that I didn't even know I was holding. I held up a finger to let Dream know to give me a sec, before walking away from the table.

"Hey, baby-."

"Didn't I tell yo ass to beat me to the house!" Juice snapped before I could finish my greeting. Instantly my forehead bunched hearing his voice.

"Why in the hell you got Yo'Sahn's phone?" I asked walking over to the bar to order another drink.

"Cause, I knew yo hardheaded ass wasn't gone answer for me after you ain't do what I told you to, now where you at?" he sounded mad as hell, and I couldn't even hide the giggle that bubbled up in my throat. "What the fuck you laughing at, you drunk?"

"Naw I ain't drunk, and I'm laughing at yo crazy ass! I don't know what makes you think you my boss nigga, but you don't tell me what to do."

I rolled my eyes up into my head and waved the bartender over since she was acting like she ain't see me. Juice was getting on my nerves. I didn't even understand why he was pressing me so hard about going out. Yo'Sahn was old enough to watch himself, so he didn't have any reason to be rushing me home.

"Oh yeah?" he chuckled like he knew something I didn't. "Well what about this, if you don't wanna get embarrassed then you better go the fuck home like I said." Smacking my lips, I finally caught the bartender's eyes and mouthed for her to bring me another double shot of Patron.

"You swear you somebody daddy. I'm not bouta play with you tonight Juice. And why the fuck you ain't tell me yo damn brother was fucking with my sister?"

"Why in the fuck would I be worried bout who that nigga fuckin- you know what don't even worry bout it. Just stay yo ass right there." I didn't even have a chance to react before he was hanging up on me. I pulled the phone away from my ear and frowned, unable to hide my irritation.

"Asshole."

A second later my drink was placed in front of me, and I guzzled it down quickly. I wasn't about to worry myself over Juice's confused ass, he didn't even want shit anyway.

It was beginning to get a little crowded, so my trip back to the table wasn't as quick as it was to the bar. A few dudes even attempted to grab my attention, but I paid their asses dust. As much as I wanted to act like Juice hadn't fucked up my mood it was clear in how I was shaking these niggas off. I was almost to our table when a strong hand gripped me around my bicep and yanked me back roughly.

"Nigga excuse y-." My words got caught in my throat when I whipped around and was met with the angry eyes of Juice.

JUICE

"*W*ha-, what you doin here?" Destiny stuttered looking around for an escape, but I wasn't letting her ass get away from me that easy. She had me out here tracking her ass down when she should've just done what the fuck I'd told her.

"Didn't I tell you I was gone embarrass you." I said, pulling her soft body into mine. "Fuck you doin' out here in this tight ass shit anyway!" I grew even more irritated, seeing how thick she was looking, and how good she smelled.

"Get yo hands off me Juice!" She tried to yank away, but I only held her tighter with a hand on the curve of her back. When I'd left the gym earlier, I'd been anticipating seeing her fine ass. After I stopped at the crib to shower, I got ready to drop Yo'Sahn off, and I hit her line. Imagine a nigga's surprise when she told me she was taking her bald head ass out for drinks. I ended up taking Yo'Sahn to my mama crib since she fucked with him heavy and then came out here to get Destiny.

"Uh, excuse you!" Some girl who I assumed was her sister because of their damn near identical features came up waving her hand all in my face. "Oh shit, my bad!" A huge grin covered her face as she looked between Destiny and me. I wasn't too worried about her anyway because I'd made sure to bring Eazy with me. She must not have caught sight of him yet though. Destiny made a feeble attempt at stopping her from walking off, but she shrugged away.

"What the fuck Dream!"

"Hey, you said you wanted dibs on Jeremiah. Welp looks like you got him boo!" Dream shouted back just as Eazy came over and enveloped her in a hug, drawing her attention away. I didn't even wait for them to walk off before I was dragging Destiny towards the exit despite her resistance. If she didn't want me to come up here, then she should've listened.

I didn't slow down my fast pace until we were out on the sidewalk, but I still held onto her hand.

"Juice! I don't even got my coat!" She huffed, trying to catch her breath from keeping up with me. I finally stopped and took in her shivering as she rubbed her bare arm.

"Shit." I'd forgotten all about her coat. Cursing lowly I took off the black, fleece and leather varsity jacket I had on, and draped it over her shoulders. It swallowed her small ass right up, making her look much more innocent and sweet than she really was. "Now bring yo ass on," I told her walking in the direction of my car. She took her time, but eventually, she followed me ducking into the passenger seat once I unlocked the doors.

"Where my baby at ?" She questioned as soon as my ass hit the seat.

"Oh, now you worried bout the lil homie? You wasn't thinkin' bout him when you decided to come out and shake yo ass." She sucked her teeth and turned towards the window, not bothering to answer me, but that was fine with me.

"How I'm sposed to get my car tho-." She tried to ask, and I cut the radio up as high as I could. I hadn't really thought about any of that shit when I dropped everything and drove all the way out here, but me telling her she could get it in the morning would probably just make her madder. So instead of saying anything, I continued to drive towards the house I had on this side of town.

At some point she fell asleep, and I welcomed the time to myself. I'd sped to her so fast I ain't give myself a minute to think about why I was really mad in the first place. The truth was I'd been checking for Destiny since the day I'd met her, and the shit just grew more and more intense every time I was around her ass. I'd never had a bitch dominate my thoughts the way she did. She had me out here doing shit for her I would never do and had never done for any other female. I'd even checked I'yanna over her for that bullshit she pulled, I mean she sucked my dick afterwards, but I definitely let her know to back off Destiny. Me pulling up on her tonight was the first time I'd ever felt the need to track a bitch down. Like legit I used Yo'Sahn's find my iPhone app so I could find her. I shook my head at how thirsty I was acting as I looked over her features. Even though she was supposed to be relaxed in her sleep, her forehead was scrunched up, and her lips were pushed out into a cute pout. I knew it was cause she called herself having an attitude with me, but I had to stop myself from reaching over and smoothing out the crease in her brow.

Focusing my attention back in front of me, I navigated my way through the damn near empty streets until I pulled into my driveway electing not to park in the garage.

"Aye get up." I shook her awake and got out, making sure to slam the door shut. When I walked around she was still sitting inside with her seatbelt on talking shit, but we were already here, and I wasn't taking her ass nowhere else. By the time I made it to my door she'd gotten out and was stomping up behind me.

"Juice! Juice I know yo black ass hear me!"

"Yeah, I hear you and so do every-fuckin-body-else. Stop

screaming like that over here." I spat looking at her ass crazy. This neighborhood wasn't no super rich, exclusive one, it was more middle class, but I ain't want her waking nobody up. It was old people in just about every house over here, and despite them being labeled as nosy I hadn't had any problems out of any of them. I rarely came out this way anymore, though. When I bought it a few years ago, I would spend the entire weekend over here every weekend just so I could get some peace and quiet. The more business picked up, the less I came through since I didn't have the time. Only our parents knew about this spot because I hadn't told Eazy. He loved trying to lecture me about being responsible and growing up, but I'd already been doing my own thing. Just because a nigga liked different hoes occasionally didn't mean I didn't wanna grow as a man. I just wanted to do shit on my own, and I had been. That's another reason why I'd been fucking with I'yanna the way that I had. She had put me on to some investments and a whole apartment building that I owned. Eazy thought I was just out here on some dumb shit, but I was getting legit money too.

"Don't tell me to be quiet when you basically just kidnapped me! And where the fuck my baby at? You all worried about me going out and now he at the house alone and my damn phone dead." She said in an annoyingly high pitched voice, adding all that neck rolling and finger snapping that females liked to do.

"Mannn I ain't bouta argue with yo bald head ass, Yo'Sahn fine where he at trust me. He gone be well taken care of." I let us inside, and she stormed past me but stopped in her tracks at what I said.

"Nigga what!" She asked cocking her head, and it was almost like I could see her mind working in overdrive. "You bet not had left my son with one of your bitches!" I hadn't never seen no female ready to turn up as fast as her, but I was far from the nigga Dre and she wasn't about to whoop my ass.

"Don't try and play me like a lame. That's fuck boy shit." I checked her. "He with my OG, his lil ass stay up under her since he found out she cook other shit besides noodles and pizza for dinner," I smirked at the way her face dropped and strolled past her to the leather sectional in the middle of the room while she recovered. She stood in the same spot while I switched my 75-inch tv on to ESPN.

"So?" She dragged trying to get my attention after a few minutes. "Where I'm sposed to sleep?" Attitude was heavy in her voice, only making the situation more comical to me.

Without tearing my eyes away from the screen, I pointed her to where the guest bedroom was. Honestly, I needed a minute away from her ass so that I could get my thoughts together because now that I had her here, my mood had definitely shifted and I wasn't even mad anymore. The second she disappeared towards the back I grabbed a blunt and some weed out of the box I had stashed under my coffee table. It was always easier for me to sort through shit when I was high and I damn sure needed to get a handle on my damn feelings for Destiny. I could admit that she would be a perfect fit for me if I were open to something serious, but I wasn't. Plus shorty had some baggage with her that I didn't want to carry. I fucked with Yo'Sahn, but did I want to be the nigga's stepdaddy? Where the fuck was his real daddy even at? For all I knew she'd run him off doing that ratchet baby mama shit, or worse he was still in the wings waiting for another shot. Then I couldn't forget about her messing with a bum ass nigga like Dre. She may have been a thorough chick, but I couldn't let the fact that she'd even fucked with his snake ass slide. It was a lot of shit with Destiny, and it constantly fucked with my ability to go there with her, but sometimes I couldn't help but stare at her fine ass. I imagined fucking her more often than I should have, and every time I caught myself, I'd get a whole fucking attitude. I finished rolling my blunt and sparked it up immediately feeling its calming effects as it took my mind off shorty.

Almost an hour passed and I had finished the one blunt and rolled another right after. I was halfway through the second one and watching the game highlights when Destiny eased her way back into the room. I lazily glanced up at her and eyed her chocolate thighs that were barely covered by one of my graphic tees. Her skin was looking smooth and shiny like she'd moisturized with coconut oil. I licked my lips but didn't say nothing as she plopped down next to me smelling all sweet and shit like Dove body soap.

"I couldn't sleep in there alone." Was the first thing she muttered once she'd taken a seat.

"Don't you do it at home?" I said, turning back to the tv in an effort to tame the stirring in my joggers. She looked like straight up temptation sitting over there with her hair pulled up and dressed in only a t-shirt. I filled my lungs with another hit of loud instead of pulling her into my lap like I wanted to.

"Why you always being an ass? Remember you're the one that brought me here the least you could do is keep me company." She replied smartly snatching the blunt from between my lips and taking a long toke of her own.

"Can't be that bad, you brought yo ass out here fuckin' with me. I'm bouta go to bed though anyway. Let the tv keep yo ass company." I stood and headed to the back where my room was, leaving her there with her mouth dropped open. Destiny knew exactly what she was doing coming out there like that, and I was trying not to take it there with her. I closed the door behind me once I made it to my room and stripped down to my boxers and tank top before laying down on top of the blankets. I needed to cool the fuck off before I did some shit I was gone regret. It wasn't until my eyes closed that I realized how tired I really was, because I dozed off quick as fuck.

Someone climbing on top of me instantly had my eyes snapping open, and I jumped up only to hear Destiny talking to me in a hushed tone as she pressed her naked body into mine.

"It's just me!" She whispered close to my ear.

"Yo what the fuck you doing Destiny?" I frowned rubbing my eyes so that they'd adjust to the dark quicker.

"I'm tryna put this pussy on you since you won't make the first move." My dick bricked right up after she said that and was straining to be unleashed. I guess she felt that was the green light for her to go because next thing I know she's kissing me all on the neck and trying to get my dick out. No lie the shit was sexy as fuck, and my hands fell straight to her ass. She sucked my bottom lip, prompting me to kiss her deeply, as she succeeded in freeing me from my boxers.

"Aye," I pulled back grabbing ahold of her chin so that I could see her face in the dark. She never stopped stroking my dick with those soft ass hands while we made eye contact. "For real Destiny, I need you to understand what you doing. This shit ain't gone change nothin between us ayite. It's just sex." I spoke slowly hoping that she understood how serious I was about this shit. I was feeling her, but at the same time I wasn't ready to be with anybody. Let alone her. Something flickered in her eyes but it disappeared just as quickly before she nodded whispering an okay and placed me at her opening. She was so wet that I immediately felt it dripping down my dick before she even lowered herself all the way down on me. As soon as she did though I wanted to take back what I'd just said. Destiny's pussy felt like silk, and she hadn't even started moving yet. She eased down slowly, trying to adjust to my size and teasing the fuck out of me in the process.

"Sssss." I grabbed a handful of her long ass weave and pulled her head back, exposing her neck so that I could suck on it. I needed something to distract me so I wouldn't nut fast as hell, but she only moaned louder as she found her rhythm on top of me.

"Fuck Destiny," I growled out, flipping her over onto her back and lifting her legs over my shoulders. I bit down on her neck to stop myself from moaning, that's just how wet and tight she was.

"Ooooh shit! Fuck this pussy Juice!" She scratched at my back as I drilled into her changing my pace from fast to slow.

"This what you wanted, huh?" I questioned, grabbing her by the throat and giving it a little squeeze. "You needed some dick to put yo ass to sleep? You should've just said that shit!" I was talking big shit and enjoying the way her eyes were rolling in the back of her head while I stroked her faster.

"Yesss, yes I needed some diiiick!"

"You taking this shit like a pro too. Get up on them knees for me shorty."

When she turned over and tooted her ass in the air, I had to suck in a deep breath at the way her pussy had creamed. It looked like she was stashing some melted vanilla ice cream up in there and before I knew it, I'd stuck my face between her legs. I licked between her folds, then sucked her fat ass clit in my mouth, making sure to hold her thighs because of how much she was squirming.

"Mmmfuck! I-I'm cuuummming!" She screamed, shaking violently before falling flat on the bed. I wiped her juices from my face and smirked at how I'd fucked her up with the head even though I really ain't know what I was doing. With one hand I pulled her back up onto her knees and spread her legs wide so that I could play with that clit.

"Damnnn why yo pussy so good?" I muttered, slipping back in her. She squeezed her pussy muscles on me and then started throwing it back like she hadn't just tapped out a second before. There wasn't no way I'd be able to leave her ass alone after this I didn't give a fuck what I'd said. Holding onto her hips firmly, I continued to drive into her as I felt my nut rising.

"You sooo fuckin deeep Juice!" She whimpered, driving me over the edge.

"Fuuuuck I'm bouta cum, tell me where you want it?" I was panting like I'd run a fucking marathon.

"Mmmm nut in this pussy." She said barely above a whisper, and before I could stop myself, I was spreading my seeds in her garden.

"Gaaaah damnnn." I hadn't nutted that hard since I was a little nigga and the shit took me out. I was used to fucking a bitch all night, but Destiny had pulled that shit up out of me in less than an hour. Out of breath, I laid down next to her not even thinking about the fact that I'd just fucked her without a rubber. She looked over at me smiling before closing her eyes, while I was still trying to figure out what type of cocaine she had in her pussy. All my ass could do was close my eyes too, or I would've been up all night.

LOUD ASS KNOCKING WOKE me up, and I squinted at the sunlight that was splashing across my face. Looking over I saw Destiny was still knocked out beside me with drool hanging from her lips. I almost got sidetracked by her beauty but whoever was at the door was persistent as hell. Frowning I pulled the blanket up over her shoulder and climbed out of bed. I snatched a pair of basketball shorts off the chair next to my bed and made my way down the hall to get the door before whoever it was woke up Destiny. As soon as I pulled it open though I wished I hadn't because I'yanna's thirsty ass stood on the other side holding up a Tupperware dish filled with breakfast.

"Hey, I brought you some food over, can I come in and have breakfast with you?" She smiled hard and tilted her head up at me.

"Uhhh this ain't a good time-." I started making sure to check the hall for Destiny, and she used that moment to slip inside and close the door.

"Well, how about we just skip the breakfast." Before I could stop her, she dropped to her knees and tried to slide my shorts down.

"Yoooo I'yanna-."

"Just let me get a quick taste." She giggled finally freeing me. I was about to let her get a taste of Destiny since she wanted to be hard-headed. With an evil smirk, I watched her hold my shit in both hands.

"Oh hell naw!" I heard and looked up just in time to see Destiny angrily storming our way.

EAZY

I woke up to Dream yelling into the phone as she struggled to get into some sweats. Since she was facing away from the bed, I got a nice view of her ass that had me ready to pull her back under the covers with me.

"That nigga got you fucked up sis!" She screeched in disbelief snapping into a fully upright position.

Ohh shit. Was the first thing that popped into my head because I knew that we'd left her sister with Juice. I couldn't help but think that he'd done some fuck shit and now my morning was about to be ruined because of his ass. That thought was immediately confirmed when Dream spun around and glared my way.

"Listen bitch I'm on my way don't even worry bout it!" She fumed before hanging up and tossing her phone on the bed so she could finish getting dressed. I took that as my cue to get up myself.

"Aye, you gone tell me what's wrong or just keep lookin' at me all crazy and shit?" I asked once I reached the edge of the bed where she stood.

"Yo ignorant ass brother! That's what's wrong!" She tried to walk off grumbling, but I snatched her right back. I shook my head inwardly cause that nigga couldn't do shit right! There was no telling what had happened over there, but judging from how mad Dream was I knew it was fucked up. "I'm bouta go fuck him up!" She said more so to herself than to me and tried to get away again, forcing me to hold her tighter.

"Aye, calm yo ass down ayite. Whatever's going on over there ain't got shit to do with us. Now we can go get Destiny, and I might even let y'all jump Juice ass, cause ain't no tellin what that nigga did, but don't let it fuck our shit up." I told her, and the features on her face started to relax.

"You're right, my bad." She sighed.

"I already know, now gone head give me a kiss." I bent down as she stood up on her toes and our lips met. I wanted to do more but fucking around with Juice had me ending the kiss quickly and heading to the bathroom to handle my hygiene.

Fifteen minutes later I was showered and dressed in a navy blue Champions sweatsuit with some fresh out the box Air Force One's on my feet. The winter had been more cold than wet, and I was glad that it hadn't snowed the night before as me and Dream ducked into my car. I immediately headed towards my brother's crib only for Dream to stop me.

"You going the wrong way, Destiny said that they're out in Rogers Park on Ravenswood Ave." She said, looking back at her phone and texting away.

The fuck? I frowned. "You sure?" I had to ask. What the fuck was Juice doing out in Rogers Park I couldn't help but wonder.

"*Yeah, I'm sure.*" She sucked her teeth. "Destiny said they went to his house last night."

I was stuck on the *his house* part. As far as I knew Juice lived out south near our parents' crib in an apartment building. Now I was more confused than ever because I wanted to know whose crib he'd taken Destiny to. Running a hand over my waves, I took the next turn so that I could go back the other way.

With Dream's phone shooting out directions, I made it to a ranch style home on Ravenswood and squinted at the sight of Juice's car in the driveway. As soon as we came to a stop, the front door opened and Dream stormed out followed by Juice standing bare-chested with only a pair of baller shorts on and some slides. I couldn't make out what he was saying to her as I stepped out the car, but whatever it was had her yelling even louder.

"Fuck you Juice! You want it to be no feelings, ok cool, but keep that same energy my nigga!" She spat as Dream met her on the walkway.

"Mannn gone with all that shit Destiny, I told yo ass what it was, it ain't my fault you ain't believe it." He waved her off. "You wanna be out here on some thot shit I don't give a fuck just make sure you keep this shit between us cause I ain't tryna hear that shit when I come get my lil homie."

"Boy you got me fucked up if you think I'm still gone let my son be around you!" I'd just reached them when she said it and Juice's face balled up angrily.

"Just gone to the car man," I told Dream ushering them away. Juice had already started down to where we were standing, and I hurried to block his path.

"I ain't playin' with yo ass Destiny!" He barked around me, but she'd gotten the reaction she wanted out of him, so she allowed Dream to lead her away without saying anything else. "Get yo fuckin' hands off me bruh!" He shoved my hand away and stomped back to the house with me following. I took the time to look around once I'd shut the door, admiring the open floor plan and furnishings silently. It was a nice ass house, and it was obvious from the black décor and cream colored carpet that a woman's touch had been incorporated further confusing me.

"Don't come in here with that bullshit Eazy!" Juice huffed sliding down onto the couch and resting his head back.

"Nigga I ain't even said shit!"

"But you want to though, right?" He sat up with his elbows on his knees and looked my way irritably.

"Not really, I'm bouta have to listen to that shit the whole drive home. I'm just tryna figure out who crib this is."

"This my shit man." He muttered. "I been bought this spot, just on some getaway type shit." He shrugged slightly letting me know that the last thing he wanted to talk about was his living arrangements. This nigga was in denial bad. He was tryna act like whatever had happened with Destiny wasn't fucking with him, but the shit was written all over his face. Nodding I took a seat on the end of his sectional and scratched at the back of my head.

"So what happened with ole girl?" I asked.

"Nigga you said you wasn't tryna get into that."

"I mean I ain't but since whatever you did made my girl drag me out the bed I feel like you gotta at least give me the rundown." Even though he hadn't told me, it was obvious that he fucked with Destiny. The only problem seemed to be him getting in his own way, which was proven when he explained what had happened the night before and this morning.

Once he finished, I sat back and sighed heavily. "Nigga you was bouta let a bitch suck yo dick with Destiny in the back?" I asked, looking at him in disbelief.

"I mean shit, I tried to tell her ass naw, but she insisted. I figured once she tasted Destiny's cum on my shit she'd feel dumb though, but Destiny came out." He shrugged again. "That shit ain't my fault."

"It's not?"

"Hell naw! Fuck was she mad for anyway? I told her ass before we even fucked that it ain't mean shit, and she was cool. Now she acting like I said she was my bitch or something."

"Nigga-." I started, but my phone buzzed in my pocket. Without even looking I knew it was Dream's ass calling me from the car. I ignored it and sent her a text that I would be right out while Juice looked at me sideways.

"Mannn gone take yo whipped ass on."

"I ain't fuckin' whipped nigga! Just cause you in here in yo feelings, and shit don't mean I'm whipped."

"I ain't got feelings, bitch ass nigga!" He gritted.

"Yeah ayite, you the bitch. Up in here cryin' and shit like a female." I stood and started for the door before Dream pulled off in my shit. "Get at me when you get them emotions under control, we gotta talk about that nigga Budda getting out."

We still hadn't talked about Budda's upcoming release, and I still needed to figure out damage control. The mention of that nigga's name had Juice's mouth dropping open.

"What? When the fuck that nigga getting out?"

"I don't know yet, but let me get up outta here before Dream's ass pull off." I sighed, opening the door and looking out to make sure she hadn't done what I'd just said. "I'm gone get up with you." I ducked out just as she was sliding across the seat and ran over to stop her. It wasn't no way I was gone let her ass fuck my shit up, I had just got this car.

* * *

AFTER I'D DROPPED Dream and her sister off, I headed over to my parent's house to pick up Yo'Sahn with strict instructions to bring him right back. The whole time I'd been in the car with their asses I had to listen to Destiny going off about Juice and how he wasn't shit. I couldn't argue that because the stunt he'd pulled was fucked up. Her voice kept cracking, but she wouldn't come out and cry even though it was obvious she wanted to. Dream was doing her best to console her while talking her shit too, and at some point, I had to tell them to cut that shit short. My brother was a fuck up, but I wasn't about to spend a twenty-minute drive listening to their angry ass squawking. Even though the attitude was through the roof, they shut up long enough for me to drop them off at Dream's so they could get ready to head over to the shop.

"Yoooo y'all ass woke over here!" I yelled as I stepped through the door.

"Elijah watch yo damn mouth, and quit all that hollering." My mama fussed as she came around the corner, wiping her hands on her apron. The smell of buttermilk pancakes and maple syrup filled the house, and my stomach growled loudly.

"My bad ma. It smells good in here, you make me a plate?"

"Now you know I made my baby something to eat, but you better hurry up and get in there because Yo'Sahn's got the appetite of two grown men." She chuckled as I kissed her cheek.

"Mannn that lil nigga better had saved me some." I hurried past barely missing the slap she was sending my way. When I entered the kitchen, my pops and Yo'Sahn both were sitting at the table with plates piled high with pancakes, bacon, and eggs. I sat down between them and grabbed a spare plate, adding a big helping of bacon and pancakes.

"What's up pops?" I said once I was done, but he only grumbled a response since he was so busy stuffing his face. I turned to Yo'Sahn and tousled his short ass dreads. "What's good lil man, you over her conning my mama into making yo ass breakfast and shit?"

"Mannn I ain't gotta con her." He grinned slapping my hand away. "She loves me."

"She definitely got *grandbaby* fever." My dad raised his eyebrows suggestively.

"Oh, I'm workin' on that already."

"Nigga I ain't old enough to be nobody's granddaddy yet!" He damn near bit his tongue he gritted so hard. Me and Yo'Sahn laughed while he just mean mugged me as he chewed.

"Elijah, you know damn well you're more than old enough for grandkids. We got two grown ass sons, who are perfectly capable of blessing us with the sound of Lil feet running around here." My mom reprimanded him quickly.

"Hell naw! Yo'Sahn already got that covered for now, ain't that right son?" My dad quizzed looking across the table at Yo'Sahn, who couldn't hide his grin.

"Yup!" Cheesing he stuffed a fork full of food in his mouth. I couldn't even do shit but laugh myself. It was cool that my folks had gotten so close to him, especially since I planned on getting serious with his aunty. Besides how we'd met, Yo'Sahn was a cool little dude, and I liked having him around. Not only was he smart as hell, but he was talented. The little nigga could out ball all our asses, and I wasn't just saying that. I was glad I'd been able to intervene when he was trying to jump into the street life, and with how much time we'd been spending together he was starting to make me wonder about the type of influence I was to him. I wouldn't say that I was ready to give up the game yet, but I damn sure was thinking about other kids that I allowed on this fucked up path.

Not too long later we'd said our goodbyes to my parents and were on the way to drop Yo'Sahn off at school with full stomachs. I wasn't about to take him all the way home just for him to end up riding the bus to school all because Destiny had an attitude. Plus, I didn't want him to be privy to the fact that something had happened between Juice and his mama. He looked up to Juice and had been spending just as much time with him as with me, so I knew that he wouldn't take the new *restrictions* well. Besides when Juice dropped him off he already had a change of clothes with him, so taking him home was just Destiny being petty and I wasn't about to play into that shit.

I eyed him while he looked for a song to play on his phone, before he settled on some, NBA Youngboy and sat back in his seat bobbing his head.

"Aye Juice still picking me up, right? He sposed to take me to the court so I can work on my layups before tryouts." He asked, looking my way.

"Oh, yeah? You tryin' out for basketball and ain't tell me?" I feigned hurt and steered the conversation away from Juice. I wasn't trying to be the one that had to tell him that his mama might not let that shit go down. Knowing Juice, he'd show his ass if he had promised to take him and Destiny acted up.

A slow grin spread across his face, and he shook his head shyly. "Nawww man, I was gone tell you after I made the team and shit-, *stuff.*" He stopped himself from cursing. "I just wanted to make sure I'd get a jersey first."

"What! You already know you gone be in the starting line up. If that coach don't pick you he a damn fool!" I said, tousling his hair.

"Yeah Juice said he'd shoot his ass if he didn't!" He laughed while shaking his head and smoothing down his locks. Usually, I would've been annoyed that Juice had told him some shit like that, but it was obvious lil dude was enthralled with that nigga. If him and Destiny ain't work their shit out, he would for sure be crushed.

"Well lucky for him you got skills, so ain't gone be no need for that," I told him as I pulled up in front of his building. There was a ton of kids out waiting on the bell to ring, and they all looked our way thirsty as hell to see who was pulling up in a Cullinan. I spotted his friend out of the crowd, standing next to some niggas that were too damn old to be out at a grammar school, rocking a red hat and banging it to the left. When he saw us in the car, his face immediately turned cold, and I put a hand on Yo'Sahn's shoulder stopping him from exiting.

"What's up with yo lil homie?" I wondered nodding in his direction. When he realized who I was talking about, he shrugged and hoisted his bag off the floor.

"He been on that bull shit-, we ain't cool like that no more, since Juice said I need to watch him. Plus he hanging with them niggas now." I could tell it bothered him, but being the type of kid he was, he wouldn't say nothing. From the hard mug he was sending our way though I agreed with Juice and I made a mental note to put somebody up on Yo'Sahn to make sure he was good out here when we weren't around.

"Yeah stay away from his lil ass and let me know if he gives you any problems." I kept my eyes on the boy as I spoke to Yo'Sahn. Even little niggas like that needed to be watched, and I wasn't gone take a chance. If I didn't have some business to attend to then, I would've felt the need to stay and make sure he was straight, but I was definitely gone have somebody keeping tabs. Yo'Sahn nodded without arguing and got out while I watched him closely until he disappeared into the building and pulled off with my phone in hand.

DREAM

$\mathcal{I}$t had been a few weeks since the whole Destiny and Juice situation and let me tell you they were both being just as stubborn as an ox. While she had changed her tune about him seeing Yo'Sahn, she was very adamant that somebody else would need to make the exchange. She was real life acting as if they were divorcing parents with a small child. I just couldn't take her seriously. Now while I can admit that Juice was lowdown for what he'd done, I felt like *she* should have known better. Especially after she'd run down how he messed with Makalah, and the fact that he'd told her *before* having sex that it would not make them a couple. At the end of the day though she was my sister, so I was riding with her right or wrong. However, despite his lack of respect, he was good as fuck with Yo'Sahn and had been an excellent role model for him.

Now, on the other hand, Elijah and I had been getting along great. Without even trying I'd gotten into a whole relationship, and it had been nothing short of amazing. I'd never been with anybody like him before and I'd definitely never been treated better. He gave me just the right amount of atten-

133

tion, enough to know he cared but not so much that I felt smothered. We had romantic ass dates and sometimes we just chilled which always seemed just as special as the dates we went on.

How well he treated me was a big part of the reason why I didn't stop fucking with him once Destiny finally slipped up and explained how she'd met them during one of her rants. It did explain a lot though considering that I'd gotten thug vibes from his ass since the moment we'd met. At this point though it was all null and void because I was in too deep. Elijah was turning me straight out, and while it was way too soon to say I loved him, I knew that's where things were headed. I'd had dinner with his parents, and we'd been doing more and more overnights.

Since the contractors were still fixing his house, he'd finally broken down and gotten an apartment for the time being so that we didn't always have to sleep in a hotel room when I stayed over and I had to admit it was nice as hell. His bed was much more comfortable than mine, and I often found myself wanting to stay there more than at home.....just like I'd done this morning.

"Dream yo ass got it bad, over there daydreaming and shit! I don't blame you though cause if I had a man like that I'd be stuck in Lala land too." Sariah's ratchet ass called out loudly. We'd been working with the girls for about a month, and although Sariah and Gabby were ghetto and extra as fuck. They both brought in a lot of clientele and could work their way around a head.

Ashley and Danielle were somewhat more professional as far as how they behaved in the workplace, and we'd been getting along with them great. Those were my girls, and I was glad that we'd kept them on. After we got the sign redone and our name out there, it hadn't taken long for us to get a lot more women coming in for wig and lash treatments since it was a new service and very much in demand. Yeah, *Lashes & Lace* was doing well, and I couldn't have been happier.

"Girl if you had ANY man you'd be stuck ole thirsty ass!" Danielle chimed in causing us all to laugh even the customers and Sariah to suck her teeth.

"You talkin' like you ain't single as a dollar bill tho! I still ain't never seen you with no nigga, I'm starting to think you like the same thing they do!" Sariah put two fingers up to her mouth and slithered her tongue like a snake.

"Oooh!"

"Oh no she didn't!" Customers began hooting.

"If I was I'd STILL get more play than you tho!" Danielle shot back slapping hands with Ashley. Unable to think of a quick come back Sariah waved her off with a dry ass "whatever" before returning to her client's head like she should've been doing in the first place. I was glad Ms. Rachel wasn't there to hear them talking like this. Even though she was used to them bickering, I still wasn't comfortable indulging in certain shit while she was around considering my relationship with Elijah. I wanted to make a good impression on her, so I was keeping the ratchet shit to a minimum.

The bell chiming over the door drew all of our attention that way, and I released a heavy sigh as my mama stepped inside dressed in some dark blue skinny jeans and a fluorescent hoody. I couldn't deny that she didn't look a day over forty, but the alcohol was definitely beginning to takes it's toll.

After a minute or two she started getting all loud with the receptionist, and I knew I'd have to intervene. Excusing myself from my client, I started over and tried to prepare myself for the bullshit.

"I just told yo simple ass I don't got no appointment! This my daughters' shop- why I'm even talkin' to you! Dream! Destiny!" She started yelling and looking around until her eyes landed on me. "See! Dream tell this bitch I'm yo mama!" She pulled her purse strap higher onto her shoulder and smirked at Claire whose face was tight as hell.

"I'm sorry about this, Claire, I'll take it from here. You can go ahead and go to lunch." I addressed my employee first since she looked like she was ready to go upside my mama's head. She gave a look of gratitude before grabbing her things and heading towards the door.

"You don't gotta apologize to bitches that work for you Dream." My mama spat rolling her eyes. "See Destiny would've had my back, you so damn bourgeois."

Pinching the bridge of my nose, I started counting backwards in an effort to control the anger I felt brewing in my gut. Her breath reeked of liquor despite her trying to cover it up with Listerine. That let me know that she was already amped and ready to go so this conversation wouldn't end well, not that I was really expecting it to.

"What do you want ma? This is my place of business, and I can't have you up here acting a fool." I hissed lowly and checked to make sure nobody was paying attention, but after the big ass scene she'd caused all eyes were glued to us.

"First of all, watch how the fuck you talkin' to me, I'm still YO mama! And secondly why ain't you tell me you was opening a business? You swear you're too good to talk to me!"

"Ughhhh you're doing the most," I was already tired of the back and forth and wished she'd just get on with her reason for being there. It could only be for a handful of things, and I was willing to bet it had something to do with money.

"Fine! Let yo mama hold something, and don't say you ain't got it cause I know *somebody* done paid you already." She bucked her eyes at me as she held her hand out, proving exactly what I'd been thinking.

"I should've known that's all yo ass wanted-."

"Well it's the least you could do Dream La'Shay! It ain't like you hurtin' for it!" She had the nerve to frown at me like I wasn't shit before adding. "Can't even give yo own mama some money."

"Hmph sure can't," I grunted rolling my eyes.

"That's a damn shame." She sucked her teeth then went into her purse, handing me an envelope. "I only came to give yo lil nappy head ass this! You lucky Budda already paid me!"

I was so shocked by the mention of Budda's name that I didn't even try to stop her when she switched away. Turning the envelope over in my hand, I saw that it was indeed from my ex, and I found myself frowning in irritation. I'd made it more than clear that I didn't want nothing to do with him. Obviously, me blocking his jail calls wasn't getting my point across so the nigga sent a message through my mama. The letter clearly had my name with her damn address since he didn't know mine. And it had already been opened, by my mama's nosey ass. Swallowing the lump that had formed in my throat, I sat down at the desk and started reading to see exactly what this nigga had to say.

Of course it was filled with nothing but the usual jailbird talk. *I love you. I'm sorry. I've changed, and I'm trying to do right by you this time.* Blah. Blah. Blah. What I wasn't prepared to see though was that he'd be returning from prison soon. Like within the next month or so soon. And not only that but he'd sent me a check for five hundred dollars which was supposed to be included, but it was obvious to me that, that was the money my mama had been talking about. It wasn't like I would have accepted it anyway, but her ass ain't have no business taking it. I'd let her make it though because I didn't want shit from Budda and I planned on going to tell his ass just that. I was happy with Elijah and I didn't want him coming around ruining anything I had going on. As hard as it would be to see him, I was going to go up there dressed like a million bucks and glowing like the sun, just to let him know exactly how done we were. I just hoped that Elijah didn't find out.

* * *

THE SHOP WAS FINALLY CLOSED and Destiny who'd arrived a few hours before sat in the office with me, listening while I gave her a rundown about the day's events. After the other girls had left, we ordered some Chinese food and I cracked open my emergency stash of wine coolers that I kept in my trunk.

"Ok, so fuck his cockeyed ass!" Destiny scoffed once I'd finished, taking a sip of her fuzzy navel flavored drink. She didn't know about all that I had endured messing around with Budda, so she figured if I ignored him, then he'd go away, but that was so far from the truth. The fact that he was still trying to contact me when I'd basically been refusing him all these years was proof that his ass was delusional and wouldn't stop. I didn't want him to get out and start up with his shit, and I also didn't want Elijah involved. For all I knew he'd try to kill him and end up in jail himself.

"It's *been* fuck him, and he should know that by now, but he don't. So, I'm just going to go up there and tell him myself."

Her eyes bucked instantly, and the contents of her mouth spewed out onto the desk. "Bitch is you crazy! *Eazy* gone kill both y'all ass!" She resorted to calling him by his street name, which I'd been refusing to do and hated when anybody else did, which is why I gave her a side-eye. "*My bad Elijah,* gone kill both y'all ass!" She corrected, rolling her eyes.

"Not if he don't know he won't."

She shook her head in disagreement. "See, you still think you fuckin with a regular ass nigga."

"Girl-."

"Ayite he gone show you better than I can tell you. At least you got the brother that care enough to fuck you up." Sadness clouded her face as she sat back taking another drink. I hadn't really seen her display any other feelings about her and Juice's situation besides anger. So for her to sound so down about it had me a little surprised. I'd been around him a few times, and Juice or *Jeremiah* was nothing like my man. It was hard to even tell the two were brothers. While I had yet to see Elijah's rougher side, it seemed like that's all I saw with Jeremiah unless of course my nephew was around. Other than that the nigga was rude as hell and didn't care what came out of his mouth. Still, I immediately felt for my sister, seeing how his lack of caring bothered her.

"So, y'all still not talking?" I asked with hiked brows.

"Nope. And I ain't tryin' to either. Fuck him." Just that fast she'd put back on her *I don't give a fuck façade.*

I rolled my eyes at her flip-flopping ass and finished off my bottle. "Yeah you are that's why you brought him up in the first place, but gone head and keep lying to yourself."

"Ain't nobody worried bout Juice, as long as he's there for Yo'Sahn, I'm cool." She was full of shit, but I wasn't about to keep pushing her. At some point, she was going to have to admit it to herself that she cared about him.

"How is the basketball star doing anyway?" I hadn't had a chance to catch up with him for about a week since he was either at practice or with Juice and Elijah living his best pre-teen life.

"He's great," she cheesed, her mood instantly lighting up. "His first game is on Friday, and he's extra excited. You guys gonna come right?"

"Hell yeah and I'm bringing some signs too," I told her with a wink. From what I'd been told Yo'Sahn was a natural, so I was excited to see him play.

"I'm getting some jerseys and shit made too bitch! He gone be embarrassed as hell!" We shared a laugh at how he was going to react. Yo'Sahn was growing up, and his mama and aunty at his game showing out was sure to have him in his feelings. As we continued to talk about the upcoming game a text from Elijah came through. I couldn't help but smile at his message, telling me he'd be over after he finished up his business.

"Ugh, y'all make me sick," Destiny said sucking her teeth.

"Don't hate hoe." I stuck my tongue out at her playfully. "Now help me get this shit cleaned up so I can go meet bae." I was already picking up our food containers as I spoke because I was more than ready to see Elijah even though we'd just been together that morning. Destiny grumbled as she helped, but I was just glad she'd let go of trying to talk me out of seeing Budda. That was happening no matter what she said, I just hoped that it went well.

DESTINY

$\mathcal{I}$ pushed a cart around the grocery store making sure to grab enough snacks and drinks for Yo'Sahn. It was like he grew overnight, and his appetite had picked all the way up. Since I wasn't running from one job to another, it gave me more time to cook, but I still grabbed him some pizza, pizza rolls, hot pockets and other things that he could make himself on the days I didn't feel like getting in the kitchen.

"Ma did you grab some Flamin' Hots?" Yo'Sahn who'd been all in his phone since we got there finally looked up long enough to ask. He had all of his daddy's features, and I swore for a second it was Antonio's no good ass talking to me.

"Naw, you can go get them, but hurry up cause I'm ready to check out." I barely had the whole sentence out before he ran off to the chip aisle. This was supposed to be a quick store run, but we'd been there for more than an hour, and I was ready to take my ass home. I spotted some peach yogurt and reached to grab a couple when someone clearing their throat got my attention.

Turning around, I was shocked and slightly aggravated to see Dre's grandma. Since he had stolen my money I'd cut off all ties with him, including the calls from her number. His ass always resorted to calling me from other phones whenever I stopped answering or blocked him altogether.

"*Destiny.*" She twisted up her mouth like she'd tasted something sour, making her look even crazier since she didn't have her dentures in. Me and Ms. Taylor had never gotten along. For whatever reason she didn't like me from the moment Dre brought me to her house, and the feeling was mutual. She always wore a crooked ass, nappy wig and a bright colored muumuu that swallowed her bony little body up.

"*Ms. Taylor.*" I quipped matching her tone. Placing my yogurts in the cart, I began to walk away, but she grabbed ahold of my arm stopping me.

"I know why you ain't been answering my calls!" Her eyes narrowed at me suspiciously.

Rolling my eyes, I snatched out of her grasp. "I don't know-."

"Don't lie to me you little bitch! You did something to Dre didn't you! I know you did!" I was still stuck on the fact that she'd been the one calling me. Now she was accusing me of *hurting* him? To say I was confused was an understatement, but more than that I was pissed!

"Look I don't know what the fuck you're talking about! The last time I heard from yo dog ass grandson was when he stole my damn money!"

"Hmph! Is that why he's missing then! He told me about that hoodlum you cheated on him with! I just want you to know that whatever y'all did with my Dre the police will find out about it! You're lucky I ain't forty years younger, or I'd beat yo ass myself!" She fumed loudly drawing the attention of a few workers and some of the other customers that were close by. I pinched the bridge of my nose to try and calm myself down because I was five seconds away from putting this old bitch on her ass.

"Ma, you straight?" Yo'Sahn appeared out of nowhere with his face balled up. He had the same disdain for Ms. Taylor that I did because every time she saw him, she had some slick ass shit to say. I used to think that it was just because she didn't like me, but I soon realized that it was because Dre was over there badmouthing him to her. She was actually lucky that he'd walked up. Yo'Sahn's presence was the biggest reason I had decided right then not to go upside her head.

"She's fine besides the fact that she's a murdering lil whore! Yo lil bad ass was probably involved too!" She turned towards him, and before I could stop myself, I pushed her back away from him. It wasn't even that hard, I just wasn't about to have her put her hands on my kid, but of course she milked that shit. I watched in horror with everyone else as she held her chest and yelped like Fred Sanford.

"Oh my God, ma'am! Are you okay?" A chorus of concern rose around us as people rushed to her aide, and I took the opportunity to pull Yo'Sahn away. I'd been completely caught off guard by that whole scene, and as mad as I was about the way she just came at me the question still lingered. *Where was Dre?* It wasn't surprising that he'd disappeared after stealing from me, but that nigga had to be dead to not be in touch with his grandma. And for some odd reason, I couldn't help but think his disappearance had everything to do with a certain *King* brother.

On the way home, I stopped to grab some McDonald's for Yo'Sahn since I didn't have much of an appetite anymore. I could tell that he wanted to ask me what was going on, but thankfully he knew better because I didn't know how to explain the shit anyway. Juice had put me in an awkward position with this shit, so once I knew that Yo'Sahn was asleep, I called him only to be ignored. It dawned on me to text him from Yo'Sahn's phone after being sent to voicemail two more times.

Me: hey can you come get me?

I watched as the bubbles popped up on the screen and was glad that Eazy had gotten him a new one. The screen was so fucked up on the old phone that I didn't know how he never cut his fingers texting. Finally, after damn near five minutes, he hit me back.

Juice: stop fuckin playin' with me Destiny, yo ass ain't slick

I sucked my teeth, something that was turning into a habit every time I talked to his ass and let him know that it was important and that it was about Dre. He must have understood what I was trying to say because he replied quickly that he was on his way. His ass showed up not even ten minutes later, letting me know that he was already out when I'd called. For some reason, him being out in the streets had me annoyed as hell, and when I laid eyes on him it was even worse.

Juice stepped into my living room smelling good enough to eat and looking even better. As usual he was dressed down in a dark gray, Balmain pullover, black lightly distressed jeans, and some black Tom Ford sneakers. He wore his hat down low over his eyes, but I could see that he'd recently visited the barber from how crispy the lining in his beard was. I shuddered thinking about how it had tickled my thighs when he'd tasted me, and I looked for something in the room to distract me.

"Aye man, don't text my phone mentioning that nigga name." Was the first thing out of his mouth, taking me right out of my lustful thoughts.

"What did you do Juice?"

His usual mean expression turned colder as he advanced on me. "I don't know *what* you talkin' bout shorty. I ain't did shit."

"Well, Dre's ugly ass grandma begs to differ." I kept my voice low so as not to wake Yo'Sahn. "She came up to me at the grocery store in front of my son talkin' about *I* did something to him loud as hell."

"Fuck that bitch! You ain't did nothin,' so you ain't got shit to worry about." He shrugged like I hadn't just told him I was accused of murder today in front of a store full of people. If that

144

bitch wanted to, she could bring some serious problems my way, and with Juice around Yo'Sahn, it would bring those same problems to him. As much as I disliked his ass right now, I didn't want him going to jail over Dre. It was crazy that I was ready to protect a man I'd just met over one I had spent years with, but in the short amount of time that Juice had been around my life had changed for the better. All Dre ever did was mooch and treat me and my son like crap. After he'd stolen from me money I'd saved for something so important I was done with his ass, and as mean as it sounded, I wasn't too pressed about him being dead.

"But-."

"But nothing. Look… if she starts doing too much talkin' then I'll go take care of it." His tone let me know exactly what he meant. Given the circumstances, my panties shouldn't have been as wet as they were. This man was literally standing in front of me saying that he was going to "take care" of an old lady and that he'd done the same to my ex. None of that seemed to matter as I looked into his dark eyes. He was so damn hand-some, and despite the bullshit, I always felt safe when he was around. "Was that it?" He asked, already turning to leave.

Chuckling dryly, I nodded. "I guess so." I was brought back to reality that fast. It had been a mistake to think that the reason he was doing this was because he gave a fuck about me. He'd made that point time and time again, and I was still holding on to hope like an idiot.

Oblivious to my hurt feelings, he went and opened the door. "Come lock up." He said, not even waiting for me before darting out.

"Ugh, I hate him." I stomped angrily locking the door like he said, wishing that I could slam it too. Once again I'd made myself look foolish, fucking around with Juice, but it would damn sure be the last time that I did.

* * *

FRIDAY ROLLED AROUND MUCH FASTER than I thought it would and I had spent the entire week working from morning to night. Not that it was extremely hard work doing lashes and eyebrows, but with the new specials we were running doubled my clientele. Damn near every stylist's customers wanted my added services, plus I was doing simple hairstyles too. I was deep in my bag and trying to keep my mind off of Juice. Working had helped some, but not having to physically see him or I'yanna made it that much easier. At Yo'Sahn's game though there would be no way to avoid him. If he were in the same building as me no doubt I'd be ogling him, whenever I wasn't tuned in to the game. Since me and Dream were both going, Ms. Rachel stayed at the shop with the girls, because she just didn't trust that they wouldn't kill each other without one of us being there. I could definitely understand that because between Sariah and Gabby I didn't know who was worse, they stayed starting shit with Ashley, Danielle, and Claire. The bitches were lucky they were good at what they did and better than any of the people that had applied so far, but I was hoping that wouldn't always be the case. I couldn't stand those bitches.

Before heading to the school, we took Yo'Sahn to Olive Garden for something to eat since he loved their chicken alfredo. While we ate, I had a couple cocktails with Dream to try and loosen myself up because I was a nervous wreck at the thought of seeing Juice. By the time we finished though I was much more relaxed. We took a few pictures so that we could show off our matching, maroon, and white jerseys with the same number as Yo'Sahn. Since he loved Lebron and Jordan, he had been extra geeked about getting the number 23. Let him tell it, it was his lucky number these days. Not too long after we were pulling up to Sutherland Elementary, and it was packed.

"Come on, Elijah said he saved us some seats." Dream gushed

once we got inside and Yo'Sahn went to the locker room. I allowed her to pull me towards the gym, where people were flowing in and out. We squeezed through the crowd, and she quickly pointed out Eazy and Juice sitting high up on the bleachers. They were both easy to spot amongst the sea of people in attendance. Not only were they fine as hell, but they looked like money. That alone had every bird in the building, trying their hardest to get their attention. I mean even women who looked twenty years older than us were trying hard to be seen. Rolling my eyes, I followed Dream to where they were sitting.

"Hey baby, sup Destiny." Eazy stood up to greet Dream with a hug and kiss while Juice's rude ass remained seated and barely gave us a head nod. There was no room to move past them as they caked on the bleachers, so I ended up sitting next to Juice, unfortunately. Eazy had let Dream talk him into rocking a jersey like us. Since the weather was permitting today, he didn't have on a shirt underneath, and his muscles were all out and glistening. Paired with dark jeans, some timbs and a white hat he was drawing all types of envious stares my sister's way. He only rocked a gold Rolex and a thick Cuban, but you could tell his ass was ballin'. Juice had already let me know that he wasn't about to do all that since he had plans after the game and had instead opted on a maroon hoodie, light wash jeans and some retro "red velvet" Jordan's. With his sleeves rolled up, you could clearly see the Patek on his wrist shining and so was the diamond stud in his ear. Once again he had his hat pulled down low over his eyes, but the second that Yo'Sahn's team came out he pushed it up so that his thick curls were visible, further adding to his appeal. I tore my eyes away and grabbed one of the many signs Dream had snuck in without Yo'Sahn seeing and held it up.

"Yo'Sahn! That's my baby!" I shouted out his name, and he looked up, clearly embarrassed.

"Aye man sit yo ass down they ain't even doing shit but warmups." Juice frowned at me. Realizing that I was the only person standing up and screaming, I sat down salty as fuck while Dream chuckled.

"Bitch that shit ain't funny."

"Yeah it was hoe, don't be mad at me cause you in here embarrassing my nephew and yourself." She wasn't lying, but that didn't stop me from sticking my tongue out at her. I didn't know shit about basketball besides Shannon Brown, and that was only because of him being married to Monica, and I saw a few of Lebron's "taco Tuesday" posts on the Shade Room. Other than that, I was out of my element. I sat down and pulled my phone out to busy myself while the team warmed up and immediately logged onto Facebook. There was a ton of likes under my photo from earlier and just as many comments, all noting how good I looked. I clicked back to my newsfeed and was randomly liking posts when a message popped up from Jaceon Mills a nigga I went to high school with.

I bit my lip as I looked over his profile picture. It was a close up, and he still looked just as good as I remembered. He was very light-skinned, with dark eyes and kissable pink lips. Back in high school, he wore his curly hair faded on the sides with a silky ponytail on top, but now it was low cut all around and full of waves. He looked good as hell still, and I couldn't stop the grin that spread across my face. I let a few minutes pass before I messaged him back a simple "hey".

We caught up for a few until the buzzer sounded alerting me that Yo'Sahn's game was starting. I let him know that I was at my son's game and he gave me his number with instructions to hit him up when it was over if I wasn't busy. After I promised to stay in touch, I put my attention on the game. I'd been so into the conversation that I hadn't realized Juice had been staring at me the whole time. When I did catch his eyes on me, he swiftly put them back on the court like he hadn't been all in my business. I ignored the evil look he was giving me and focused on the game. He had his chance, now I was over it, or at least I would pretend to be until I actually was.

Two hours later the game was over, and of course, my baby's team had won. I screamed so much that I lost my voice, but I couldn't stop grinning. Yo'Sahn had played his heart out, and I was so proud of him.

Instead of trying to fight our way through the thick crowd, we waited until the gym was damn near deserted before we finally descended the stairs in search of Yo'Sahn. Dream and I walked ahead of Eazy and Juice while I filled her in on Jaceon messaging me.

"Biiiitch! JC was a lil cutie in high school!" Dream nudged me lightly and said.

"Well, now he a BIG cutie- naw scratch that, he fine as hell with his own money too!" When we were catching up, Jaceon had told me about his barbershop and offered to cut Yo'Sahn's hair whenever I wanted. I thought that was sweet even though my baby didn't take too well to new niggas doing his lining. Besides Juice had been taking him lately and he'd grown accustomed to his barber, with his spoiled little ass.

"Good, maybe now you can keep your mind off of you-know-who." She hinted, and I rolled my eyes.

"Girl, fuc-." I couldn't even finish my sentence as a wave of nausea hit me so hard I almost couldn't hold it. Thankfully, we were passing a bathroom, and I managed to duck inside while Dream ran in behind me confused. I didn't even make it to the toilet though before everything I'd eaten came up right in front of the row of sinks. Screams erupted from the few women that were inside, as they scrambled around trying to avoid the huge mess I'd made.

"Damn Destiny I know you ain't drink *that* much." Dream crouched down and moved my hair out of my face, with a pensive look.

"I..I didn't." I panted. "It must've been that nasty ass ravioli."
My stomach flipped again, and another flow of vomit spewed
out. I could see in her face she didn't believe me, but Olive
Garden was always a hit or miss for me. Sometimes I could
stomach it, and sometimes I'd get sick, that's why I never really
took Yo'Sahn there. I figured I could make an exception today
since it was his first game and now I was regretting that shit.

"Y'all cool in there?" Eazy yelled from the other side of the
door, and I nodded for Dream to tell him we were.

"Yeah bae," she answered squinting at me. "She's cool her
stomach just didn't agree with that Olive Garden.

"More like some alcohol ain't agree with her ass." I could
hear Juice talking that smart shit and sucked my teeth.

"Ayite we bouta go grab Yo'Sahn, hit me up when y'all done."
Dream stood there grinning like a fool at how sweet Eazy was.

"Okay!" She sang happily. Since the halls were damn near
empty at this point, we could hear their footsteps fading out as
they got further away. I wiped the sweat from my forehead
since I was suddenly burning up and went to rinse my mouth
and wash my hands with Dream's help.

"What?" I asked since Dream was staring at me all hard in
the mirror. She held her hands up in mock surrender.

Grinning, she backed away. "I ain't said shit." I rolled my eyes
and finished cleaning myself up, wishing that she would get the
hell on. I knew what she was insinuating, but I wasn't even
going to entertain the thought. For one I was on birth control,
and for two, the last person I'd slept with was Juice. There was
no way God would've punished me like that….. at least I hoped
he wouldn't.

JUICE

I was making my rounds through our houses to pick up money and make sure these muthafuckas were doing what they were supposed to. Since I'd gotten rid of Savion and Gin shit had been moving much smoother out West. I knew that it was because of the example I'd made out of them niggas. That was cool with me though, the sooner they realized that I would drop a muthafucka on a whim, the better. I was much less diplomatic about shit than Eazy. That nigga probably would've tried to put their asses on probation or some shit like this was a real gig. I wasn't doing all that. The way I saw it was if you let a nigga get away with some shit once they'd try again just to see how far they could push you. There wasn't a nigga alive that had crossed me and lived to talk about it.

Me and Grim passed a blunt back and forth as I drove us to the last house before we'd go do our count. Since it was early morning, I was trying to get the shit done and out of the way because I had plans to take Yo'Sahn to the mall for some new shoes. He'd showed his ass on the courts the day before, and he deserved it. If his game hadn't ended so late, I would've taken him right after.

Since I had to do the pickups today, he ended up going home with Eazy and Dream, which worked out for everybody especially after his mama got sick. I was convinced her ass was drunk, just from the way her silly ass was acting, but Eazy really believed that bullshit about Olive Garden. He probably only fell for it because it came out of Dream's mouth. That nigga was acting real soft these days, but I couldn't deny that she was a good look for him.

My phone went off and seeing that it was my OG, I turned the radio down to answer. "Wassup ma?"

"Don't wassup ma me. Where the hell you been boy! If I gotta come find you just to see yo black ass, it's gone be a problem!" Her voice came through the speakerphone loud as hell, making Grim snicker like a bitch.

I shot him a look, and he shut up instantly. "Ma, you know I'm too damn old for you to do shit with me," I smirked.

"You ain't too old for me tho nigga!" My dad hopped on the line.

"Mannn y'all trippin-."

"Ain't nobody trippin, we just wanna *see* you." My mama came back through. They were trying to double team me and shit.

"My bad ma. I'll come through later, after Yo'Sahn and me come back from the mall."

"Oh yeah, how did his game go?" She hummed excitedly.

A grin instantly spread across my face. "Ahhh man you know my boy won that." I bragged.

"Your boy huh?"

"Ma-, you know what I meant."

"Mmmhmmm, whatever you say Jeremiah. I'm about to make him a special cake for his win, just make sure you bring him over here with your lyin' ass. Love you bye!" She rushed and hung up while I was still trying to figure out a comeback. I could tell already that she was feeding too much into the shit with Yo'Sahn. He was cool and all, but he was just the little homie. Eazy had started this shit, but I'd ended up spending more time with him only because I was the coolest out of us two and nothing else.

"Stop looking at me like that muhfucka." I snapped once I looked over and saw Grim eying me with a grin. "Whatever yo fat ass thinkin' keep that shit to yourself."

Chuckling, he looked away before hitting the blunt and handing it back to me. I wanted to hit his fat ass in the throat, but we were already pulling up to the house, so I left it alone.

An hour later we were at the counting spot, putting bills into the machine and stacking them in the safe. Eazy walked in with Trell, and they both sat down at the table.

"Aye, we need to talk about that nigga Budda." Eazy said with his face balled up.

"Shit I been waiting on you! Did you find out when he touchin down?" I glanced his way briefly and then focused back on the money in my hand.

"I've been dealing with other shit, but his release date gone be April 25th."

I stopped what I was doing and squinted as the wheels in my head began to spin. "Like in *two weeks?*" I wanted to know. As far as I knew he should've had some more years in his shit.

"Yeah nigga, two weeks and his ass freakin the fuck out." Trell added with a nod in Eazy's direction. My forehead wrinkled in confusion and irritation as I looked at my brother.

"What the fuck you trippin for?"

"It's a couple things really, one that nigga should've been doin longer than five years and two he been lyin about why he even got locked up in the first place."

"Damnnnn." Grim covered his mouth dramatically.

"Wasn't that shit like public record or something? How the fuck you ain't know?" Pissed I set down the stack of bills I'd been holding and lit one of the blunts we had rolled up on the table. I always knew it was a reason why I didn't like that nigga. Eazy used to walk around following his every word, but he always rubbed me the wrong way. It looked like he was fucked up behind this shit and as mad as I was, I felt bad for him. Basically, his mentor was a fucking snake.

"What you mean, nigga? Who the fuck would lie about some dumb shit like that?" He snapped.

"A rat!" Me, Trell and Grim all said at the same time.

"Okay so he gets out in a couple weeks, and we just get rid of that nigga." Shrugging I dumped my ash and leaned back in my chair.

"If he talkin' then we can't just kill his ass. What if he put my name on record. *Our name* nigga. We gone be the first muhfuckas they come looking for." Eazy stood and began to pace the room. He always did that shit when he was thinking.

"We gotta do something." Trell looked between the two of us.

"Just let me think ayite. I'm gone catch up with y'all niggas later."

"How the fuck you gone leave me, I rode over here with yo ass!" Eazy was already to the door by the time Trell caught up with him. That nigga had a one-track mind when he had something heavy on his mental. I just shook my head at both their asses. Eazy could try and think of something if he wanted to, but I was gone kill Budda's ass, and that would just be the end of it.

I FINISHED the count an hour later than I had intended to, but when I texted Yo'Sahn he wasn't tripping. Dream had already dropped him off at home anyway. He was just happy to be around a nigga, and I couldn't even front that shit always had my head gone. When I saw Destiny's little beat up ass car out front, I let out a heavy sigh. I'd been trying my hardest to avoid contact with her ass because I didn't want to keep seeing that look on her face. I had good intentions that morning we'd spent together, but it didn't even take me ten minutes to fuck up. That was slight shit to the damage I could do, and I wasn't trying to do her dirty. Fucking over her would be like fucking over Yo'Sahn and I didn't want his image of me tainted just because I liked a variety of pussy.

I made my way up to their door and before I could knock Destiny opened it up, looking good as hell. She was dressed in a black short sleeve dress, that stopped just above her knees and some gold sandals that showed her white toenails off. It was one of those unseasonably warm ass days since Illinois loved playing. Tomorrow it could very well be thirty degrees out and snowing, but today was a nice sixth-five with plenty of sun. I hadn't ever gave a fuck about the weather, but as fine as she was looking, I wanted to give Mother Nature a kiss for looking out. She was definitely looking better than she had the night before after she got sick.

She was glowing and shit, and looking so good that I ended up giving her more than the usual head nod. "What's up Destiny? You out here showing off them shiny ass legs today huh?"

"Heyyy Juice." She said dryly with her brows bunched together. "Yo'Sahn still getting changed but you can wait for him in here I guess." Turning on her heels, she pranced back into the living room and took a seat on the couch. She already knew what she was doing to my ass. I sat down on the loveseat and watched as she pretended to be all into her phone. It took her a few minutes, but she finally stopped smiling at her screen long enough to look up at me.

"What?" I asked finding it hard to hide my grin.

"You were looking over here." She smacked her lips.

"Shiiit you lookin good." I held her gaze, licking my lips so she remembered them between her thighs. She followed the movement with her eyes, and her mouth fell open. I knew at the exact moment that memory hit her ass cause she started fidgeting in her seat.

"Yo-Yo'Sahn! Juice is here!"

I couldn't even do shit but laugh at her ass as Yo'Sahn ran into the room with a big grin on his face. He pulled on his hoodie and dapped me up once I came to stand next to him. Destiny was still watching me clearly puzzled.

"Ima be back in a minute Ma. You want something?" He asked drawing her attention away.

"Uhhh nah, I'm good. Have fun, though."

"Ayite." After giving her a kiss on the cheek, we were out the door.

"How you feelin' superstar?" I asked as we pulled into traffic.

"I'm chillin'. It was only the first game, but I already know we gone win all them bitches!" He cheesed, and I punched his little ass in the arm.

"Watch yo mouth lil nigga you ain't grown."

"My bad, my bad."

"Right, but y'all definitely gone demolish all the other teams! You gone fuck around and get drafted if you stay focused." I told him, and I believed that shit wholeheartedly. Yo'Sahn was like the good version of me, and I found myself always trying to push him into some positive shit.

"You think so?" He squinted up at me, unsure.

"Hell yeah! You're smart, you got more skill than them other Lil niggas, plus you got Eazy and me on yo side. How can you lose?" Nodding he dapped me up, and we rode in silence for a minute while Lil Baby's *pure cocaine* flowed through the stereo.

"How yo mama doin?" I found myself asking, making him side-eye me hard before he finally spoke.

"She straight, been talkin' to some lame she used to go to school with." He shrugged looking out the window. "I just hope the nigga ain't nothin like Dre's bum ass."

I was glad he wasn't looking my way anymore because I'm sure the expression on my face would give away how tight I was to hear that shit. Sure, I had backed up off her, but between work and Yo'Sahn, I didn't see how she had enough time to be conversing with another nigga.

I reassured him that he wouldn't be because I wasn't about to let him nowhere near them. My ass was damn near ready to bust a U-turn just to go back and make sure she wasn't caking with some nigga while I had Yo'Sahn, but I shook that shit off. I'd promised shorty some new shoes, and I was going to follow through, but I was also about to get on top of this shit with her ass. Just because we wasn't fucking around didn't mean she was about to be in no other man's face. I wasn't about to have that at all.

DREAM

$\mathcal{I}$'d thought about the idea of visiting Budda for almost a week before finally making a decision. I was sure that to Destiny it seemed like my mind was made up, but really I had been going back and forth with it. Opening myself up to him was some scary shit, and it was stupid too, I could admit that. Not going and confronting him though was even more frightening. My subtle hints had been going ignored, so it was safe to assume that his crazy ass still had hope. I was going so that I could squash that hope, and maybe keep my man from doing something stupid.

In an effort to keep Elijah in the dark I'd told him I would be working all day and I'd told everybody at the salon that I would be with him. It was very tv sitcomish, but I was hoping it would work for me. Elijah should've been in meetings all day anyway after he went to check on his house. He had a club opening up and was remodeling a closed down YMCA so that he could start up his mentorship program.

I had a small window to get this done, and I was hoping to be in and out. I kept telling myself that this should be easy as I got checked in, but I couldn't stop myself from shaking, and it wasn't from the cold. In just one week Illinois had started acting like a bitch, so instead of the sundress and jean jacket I wanted to wear I was stuck in a pair of blue jeggings that had my ass looking plump. My top was a plain white bodysuit that had a mock turtle neck. Every man in the building had their eyes on me, and I couldn't say I blamed them. I was here to make Budda cry from how fine I was.

As soon as I was led into the visiting room and he laid eyes on me a wide grin covered his face, and his eyes lit up. I dodged his extended arms and took a seat at the table with a hard stare. Amused, he smirked and took a seat across the table from me, eating me up with his dark eyes.

"Damn, you look good." He gushed.

"What do you want Brian?"

His brows shot up like he was shocked by my demeanor. "Straight to the point, huh?" He chuckled leaning onto the table. I didn't even give him an answer, pursing my lips I crossed my arms over my chest and tilted my head.

"Okay, okay. You already know I want us to be together. I told you a nigga was getting out soon so I'm tryna see if we can start over." That nigga had the nerve to smile like he was offering me a big prize or something.

"Oh, really? Should I just forget about all the hell you put me through? All the hoes and mind games?" I hissed. "Keeping me prisoner in that damn house or tracking my every move! How about when you tried to make me take the wrap for those fucking drugs, huh? I don't wanna live like that no more- I *won't* live like that no more!"

"What you want me to say, Shay! I told you a million times I'm sorry! That shit was years ago! I'm different now-."

"Oh, you different now?" I mocked him with my lips turned up. "Let me guess…. You found God while you was in here? That's what you said last time, you know right before you got out and stomped my baby out of me." I moved into his line of vision since he was avoiding my eyes. I hadn't told anyone about some of the fucked up things that he'd done to me. Some of it I repressed just because it hurt too bad.

He glared my way angrily. *"Don't* fuckin test me like I won't fuck you up in here Dream!"

"You know what, fuck you! I only came up here to let you know that I'm not comin' back to you! I'm *happy*! I have a man who treats me like a queen, and he loves the ground I walk on. So when you get out-, if you get out, do not come anywhere near me. We're more than done!"

"Oh, so you gave my pussy away and think that's gone be it?" He swiped his nose, which usually meant he was mad as hell. The fact that we were in a highly secure prison was the only reason that move alone didn't have me shaking in my UGGs. Instead, I took great pleasure in knowing that if he even jumped the tall ass guards in the corner would take his ass down.

"Out of everything I just said that's all you heard?"

"I heard all that shit." He waved me off. "I'm even willing to forgive you because no matter what you sayin'. I *know* Eazy ain't fuckin you like me." I was so caught off guard by him mentioning Eazy that my mouth fell open, but no words would come out.

"Wh-wha?"

"Oh, you thought that nigga really wanted you?" Now it was his turn to smirk as he sized me up. I flinched away from his touch when he tried to caress my face. "It's cool, Shay. I'm really not that mad. I mean he wasn't supposed to fuck you, just keep an eye on you, but that's what I been saying since the beginning. You're too naïve to be out here alone without me. You can't even think for yourself."

The look on his face gave me chills, and for some reason, I couldn't help but wonder if what he said was true. Could Elijah have been playing me this whole time? Was all this shit just a game for him? As these questions floated around my head, the guards yelled out that the visit was over. I hadn't even planned on staying that long, but I was damn sure ready to go and even though I was questioning Elijah on the inside I wouldn't let Budda know he'd gotten to me. If I wouldn't risk catching a charge, I would've spit right in his face, but instead, I stood over him as he sat perfectly still, pleased with himself.

"*Fuck you Budda!*" I walked away quickly so that he couldn't see the tears in my eyes.

"You're mine, Shay! I don't care what you think, you gone always be my bitch!" He yelled at my back as I hurried out. Of course, now everybody was looking at this crazy ass nigga and me, further embarrassing me just like always. I damn sure should have listened when Destiny told me not to come because once again Budda had gotten the upper hand and I didn't feel any better. If anything I felt worse and even more paranoid than I'd been before visiting. The most fucked up part about the whole thing was that he had managed to tear down everything me and Elijah had built in a matter of minutes.

EAZY

J had been running around ever since I climbed out of
Dream's bed that morning and I hadn't stopped yet.
After meeting with a few investors about the mentorship
program, I shot over to check on the status of my nightclub and
then to my house to see how much progress they'd made on the
damage Sherice had caused. Just like last time they got to
running their mouths about it being another six months. The
street nigga in me was ready to threaten their asses, but my
business head prevailed and merely advised them that they'd
better adjust that shit or they'd be out of a job.

By lunch I was ready to call it a day, but there was other
shit I had to take care of. Not only did I need to holla at our
lawyer, but I also had to stop through and talk to Juice. The
shit with Budda still had me fucked up. I was walking around
like everything was good, but in reality, finding out that my
nigga, my mentor was on some snake shit had me looking at
everybody suspect as fuck. I'd come up under the principles
that Budda had taught me. My whole business was set up
according to the advice he'd given me. *No matter what, don't
snitch! Treat your workers fair! Never turn on your day ones.* I'd

lived and breathed that shit, and the whole time his ass was fraud.

Since Trell had come to me with this shit, I had been working overtime to make sure our shit was straight and that we weren't on the Feds or nobody else's radar. So far nothing had come up, but I was close to just going ahead and shutting shit down until I figured out what I was going to do about Budda. I hated to say it, but I was leaning towards Juice's method of just putting that nigga out of his misery. First, I had to find out what all he was involved in though. For all I knew we were reading too much into the shit and didn't have nothing to worry about, but all my years in the streets taught me to trust my instincts and my instincts were saying that shit was about to get hectic.

My phone went off letting me know my mama was calling, and I took my time sliding the bar across the screen. I wasn't in the best mood and if anybody would be able to tell it would be Rachel King.

"Hey ma," I answered, trying to sound as normal as possible.

"Hey, baby! How's your day going?" She gushed, and I could hear the sounds of the shop in the background, letting me know she was at work.

I unbuttoned the jacket on my Tom Ford suit and reclined my seat getting comfortable. "It's going good so far, I guess. Just tryna light a fire under these niggas to finish my house. How you doing, though? Y'all up in there snatching edges and shit?"

"Elijah I don't know who's worse, you or Jeremiah with that fuckin cussin'." She laughed.

"I wonder where we get it from?"

"Oh, see you tried it! You ain't gone blame that shit on me! Y'all got that shit from EJ." Shaking my head at her lying ass, I brushed a hand down my waves and chuckled.

"I'm tellin pops you over there lyin' on him and shit."

"Boy bye! That nigga knows how foul his mouth is. Anyway."

She huffed, and I could imagine her rolling her eyes. "I don't wanna mess up you and Dream's plans, but I forgot your father has a doctor's appointment and I need her to come in for maybe an hour or two. Destiny's here, but we're swamped today."

"Dream?" My grip on the phone tightened, and I pinched the bridge of my nose.

"Yes, nigga Dream! I tried calling her, but the phone kept going to voicemail-."

"Dream told you she was gone be with me?" I had to clarify just to make sure I wasn't tweaking. Fucking around with Budda I didn't know what was what these days, so before I started tearing shit up I needed to be positive I understood her right.

"Oh shit." She grumbled under her breath, and I knew my assumptions were accurate. Dream had told me that she was going to be working all day, she said that she was booked all the way up until they closed. I squeezed my eyes shut and tried to alleviate the tension I felt in my forehead. I didn't need this shit right now! Another call came through as my mama tried to explain away Dream's lies, and I rushed her off the phone, not even caring who it was. I wasn't trying to hear that shit from her. There was no need for Dream to lie to me about her whereabouts unless she was on some sneaky shit! I wasn't trying to be fucking with another lying ass female. Clicking over I saw that it was Trell calling.

"What's up bruh?"

"Aye, you ain't gone believe this shit my nigga, come over to my spot." He said quickly before hanging up. I'd put him on to find out as much as he could about the Budda situation since I didn't trust anybody else to. If he was calling and couldn't say shit over the phone, then that meant that he'd found something. I straightened up and sped out of the parking lot as questions about Dream and Budda fought for attention in my head. Both situations were serious and would need to be addressed as soon as possible, but at the moment, I needed to deal with the most dangerous one first.

Dream could be just as shady as Sherice, and as much as I loved her, I knew how to walk away from shit that didn't mean me any good. Budda though he was an entirely different story. He could fuck with my money and my freedom so that would take precedence.

I made it to Trell's crib in less than an hour and barely put the car in park trying to get out. He met me at the door with a grim look on his face holding a Manila envelope.

"Come on in."

I ducked inside, aware of how crazy I probably looked sweating and out of breath. As he led the way into his kitchen, I loosened my tie and tried to get my breathing under control. He set the folder down on top of the island and leaned over it.

"You look like shit nigga, the fuck going on?" He asked, finally taking in my appearance with concern.

I shook my head because I didn't want to bring Dream up and distract from the matter at hand. "I'm cool. Just gone head show me what you found." His face displayed unease, and he hesitated briefly before flipping open the folder.

"This is the original police report from the night Budda got knocked." Trell pointed to the first sheet of paper. I skimmed through quickly reading about how he'd gotten pulled over for swerving. It noted that he was in the car with a female and since Budda's dumb ass was acting irate and the passenger appeared to show signs of being beaten up they put him in cuffs and searched the car. In disbelief, I read how they found two kilos of cocaine in the trunk, and he immediately told them it wasn't his it was the girls. The shit that threw me for a loop though out of everything on there was Dream's name as clear as day. I released a breath I hadn't realized I'd been holding and looked at Trell who just nodded for me to keep going so I did.

After not being able to pin the drugs on Dream, Budda cut a

deal with the state to give up his team for a lighter sentence and to have his records sealed on the condition that he give up his connect and any associates upon his release. This nigga had turned on everybody, and while we all thought his guys had fallen off and just ducked out the game, he had gotten them all arrested. I flipped through the paperwork getting more and more pissed off by the second. Especially knowing that Dream had dealings with this nigga. Had she scoped me out for him? Was she being fraud this whole time? I smacked the entire stack of papers off the desk and started ramming my fists into Trell's stainless steel refrigerator until they were bleeding. Fuck what I'd said about waiting! As soon as that nigga touched down, he was dead!

"You done hulk cause that ain't it?" Trell asked once I'd stopped and was standing there breathing heavily. So far, the only thing that I was holding on to was the fact that my name hadn't been mentioned yet. As much as I would've wanted to believe that it was because Budda fucked with me I knew it was a reason and not one that benefited me.

"Gone head man!" I snapped waiting for him to drop another bomb.

"Ayite so after seeing all that shit, I figured I should check and see who been visiting that nigga. You know just because he's getting out soon and shit." He hesitated again.

"Gone head nigga spit it out!"

"Well 12 ain't been up there, but yo girl Dream went to see him today."

JUICE

J pulled up to Yo'Sahn's school to drop him off for practice. Real shit I couldn't wait to get his little ass up out my shit so I could go and snap on his damn mama. It had been some days since he told me about her talking to some nigga and I was ready to nip that shit in the bud. Call me selfish, but I wasn't ready for somebody else to come swooping in and take my woman. I'd have to work on some shit because I was still fucking Makalah, but I was willing to cut her ass off for Destiny. I didn't know if I would be willing to cut off bitches in the future, but at this moment I was prepared to.

He dapped me up and got out flossing in the latest J's. As usual, I waited to make sure he got into the building, but as soon as I saw Jayden's little nappy head ass stop him, I reached for my seatbelt. He was standing with a group of niggas, but I knew his face anywhere. Whatever he said to Yo'Sahn had him dropping his shit ready to fight, and I damn near ran over there.

"Get y'all lil asses back!" I barked stopping in front of them. They all froze up and looked my way like I was supposed to be scared or some shit. "Yo'Sahn you straight?"

He didn't answer me, he was so busy staring Jayden down with his fists balled up. "Take that shit back!"

I glanced back and forth between the two as Jayden grinned. "Make me pussy!"

"Fuck this lil nigga! Gone take yo ass to practice." I snatched his bag up and pushed it into his chest while simultaneously giving him a light shove towards the door.

"Yeah listen to yo step daddy and take yo ass on!"

"Aye, you really out here actin' like I give a fuck about you being ten nigga! Don't let these grown muhfuckas send you off! I'll let my mans beat yo ass and go to practice like ain't shit happened!" I was starting to get pissed off because I should've been gone already, but I wasn't about to leave Yo'Sahn out here by himself. It ain't take a rocket scientist to know that as soon as I peeled out, they'd try and jump him. Low key I felt like if Jayden got his ass beat real good, he might let go of this street shit, but I didn't want Yo'Sahn to have to be the one to do it. He had too much to lose while Jayden ain't have shit to be good for.

"Man fuck you!" He raised his middle fingers up at me and grabbed his little junk before running off with the rest of them clowns. When I caught his little ass, I was gone give him the ass whooping his daddy was supposed to. I made a mental note to start wearing my thickest leather belt from now on because I was sure to see him when I dropped Yo'Sahn off or picked him up. Grumbling I started towards my damn car only stopping because Yo'Sahn still hadn't gone inside.

"Them Lil niggas ain't on shit ayite gone head inside," I told him as he hesitated on the first step. He was just about to turn around and do what I said when the sound of screeching tires had us both looking towards the street where a black car was. All I saw was a flash before bullets started spraying our way. We were out in the open with nothing to cover us, so I jumped on top of Yo'Sahn and pulled out my gun. I stayed covering his body with mine as I emptied my clip into the moving vehicle. A second later you wouldn't even have been able to tell that some niggas had come through there blasting besides the thick smell of gun powder. The whole block was silent, or maybe it was the ringing in my ears that wasn't allowing me to hear shit. With pain soaring through my chest and arm, I went to turn Yo'Sahn over.

"Yo'Sahn, you straight! Aye! Yo'Sahn!" I shook him even as blood leaked from his mouth. "Yo-, Yo'Sahn!" My voice cracked, and my breathing became heavy. I was trying to fight through the pain, as a group of people ran towards us, but they were all blurry as hell, and I couldn't even make out what they were saying.

"Hold on young man. Stay with me!" Was the last thing I heard before everything faded to black.

Meanwhile inside the black car.....

"Hell yeah! Did you see that shit!" I yelled excitedly as we sped through the streets making our getaway. I was on a high right now! The only thing that would've been better was if I had gotten to see that nigga take his last breath.

"You said you was only gone shoot Juice nigga! You hit the fuckin kid too!" Grim whined like a little bitch.

"His ass was in the way! Fuck I look like not taking a clean shot cause that lil nigga was close! Yo ass sound stupid!" I lied just that quick. Yo'Sahn had been a pain in my ass since I met him. The way I saw it why not kill two birds with one stone. This shit was gone kill that bitch Destiny and I couldn't wait! It was about time them muthafuckas felt my pain. That bitch ain't give a fuck about Juice supposedly killing me, so I didn't give a fuck about taking out her little snot-nosed kid.

"Mannnn this shit ain't right!" His big ass huffed causing me to give him the side-eye. Besides him helping me get better after Juice shot me I didn't have no reason to trust him. After all, he'd only decided to help once I let him know that Juice and Eazy's reign was about to be over. When they closed the trunk on me I for real thought my ass was dead, but I only passed out.

The second Grim opened the trunk to drop my ass in a ditch somewhere I let him know that Budda was my cousin and not only was he about to hand Juice and Eazy over to the Feds, but he was about to take over. It ain't take much more convincing than that.

I was the only nigga that Budda had left out of his paper-work, and that was only because our daddies were brothers. Of course when he went down, I tried to hustle on my own before finally going to Eazy. Without my cousin around I really wasn't shit though so of course I fell off, but that shit wasn't my fault. They should've known better! Did a background check or something, but since they didn't they got hit. I knew that nigga Juice would kill me though, so I stole Destiny's money to pay them back and kept the rest for myself minus the couple hundreds I left in there. The fact that she wasn't regularly checking her money was dumb on her part.

It was obvious that her hoe ass was the reason Juice came up to the strip club on his bullshit, but what he wasn't expecting was for me to still be alive. Now his ass was the one dead or at least almost there. I'd put enough bullets in him to put 50 cent down, so I know his ass wasn't gone walk away.

"Just hit the corner and shut the fuck up!" I snapped angrily, and he did as he was told just like a good puppy. As soon as we hit the next street, I spotted the little nigga I was looking for and called him over.

"What's up!" Jayden panted out of breath once he made it to the car.

"Good lookin'," I said slipping him ten crispy hundred dollar bills. His face lit up at the sight of the money, and I had a mind to shoot his little ass too just in case he ended up talking, but instead, I tapped Grim so he could pull off. We had one more stop to make.

It took another hour to get to one of Budda's old warehouses, but the second we pulled in, and he put the car in park I sent a single bullet through the side of his head. I wasn't even moved by the amount of blood and brain matter that splashed on the window as I stepped out coolly and shut the door.

"Damn you had to kill his ass already?" Budda asked, coming from around the side of the building dressed in black.

"His ass was cryin' and shit bout Yo'Sahn. Besides how fast he turned on them niggas we ain't need his ass around no more." I shrugged.

"Facts." Budda agreed. "You ready to turn the city out?"

"Hell yeah!" Chicago wasn't gone never be the same after Dre and Budda took over......

To be continued ......

TEXT TO JOIN

To stay up to date on new releases, plus get exclusive information on contests, sneak peeks, and more...

Text ColeHartSig to (855)231-5230

Made in the USA
Middletown, DE
16 March 2021

35599270R10106